THE TOMB OF
GENGHIS KHAN

ORDER OF THE BLACK SUN - BOOK 31

PRESTON WILLIAM CHILD

PROLOGUE

THE CONQUEROR'S GRAVE

Genghis Khan was set to take over the entire world—but now he was dead. All of those strategies, those decisive victories might have been for nothing now. The empire that the Great Khan built might crumble without him, and there was a sense from all of his armies, his slaves, and his most devoted followers, that it was a real possibility. But before they could worry about the possible infighting or confusion, they had to lay there nearly unstoppable leader to rest.

Batu had been enslaved by the Mongolian Empire that Genghis Khan had stormed through his village with. He'd watched so many of the people he knew be slaughtered by the Mongolian forces but for some inexplicable reason, he had survived, though all of his freedoms had been taken away. He was forced to do whatever they wished, or suffer a bloody death if he disobeyed.

This task was no different. He was chosen by some of Genghis Khan's closest personal guard to go with dozens of slaves to a remote location that would be the Great Khan's burial place. They were told to not speak of this task they had been given. They were all dragged out from their camps in the dead of night to prepare the burial site.

Batu was used to mistreatment and went along without question. There was no point trying to fight back against them, even as they dragged him out of his tent and threw him into the line of other slaves. Hopefully, if the Mongolian Empire did fall apart without their infamous leader, their slaves would be able to slip away in all of the confusion. All Batu had to do was survive and make it to the next day—that was all that mattered. He didn't want to be dead and being prepared for burial like Genghis Khan —then again, no one would be making a grave for Batu. He would probably be left to rot wherever his corpse fell.

The journey was long and treacherous. The burial place would be naturally well protected due to the harsh environments that would surround it. Very few would be able to get to it, and even then, many were dying along the way. Over ten fellow slaves had died from falling from cliffs or from the sheer exhaustion of the trek.

The body of the Great Khan was covered in cloth and draped over the back of his horse. His personal guard walked in front of the steed, leading it along toward where Genghis Khan would be settled to rest.

Batu had no idea when they would reach their destination, but knew that it would be even more work to prepare the burial site. This was far from an easy task, but he supposed that it made sense, given the importance of it.

They journeyed through a series of mountains until they came across an enormous plateau in the midst of all of those mountain peaks. The plateau was made up of a flat faces of rock on all sides, making it impossible to walk up. They would have to climb if they wanted to get up there, and it would be a long climb.

Batu and the other slaves didn't think they would have to because there was no way they would be able to get the Great Kahn's body up there. Unfortunately, they were all proven wrong when the largest of the personal guards threw the covered corpse of Genghis Khan over his shoulder and tied it to himself with a rope, securing their dead leader's body to his person. The guard started climbing and all of the slaves watched in shock as he was actually succeeding in scaling the rock face. They all doubted that they could do it, but soon learned they didn't have a choice but to try as the other guards threatened them forward.

The slaves did their best as they slowly climbed up the plateau. The rocks weren't very easy to hold onto as many of them were sharp and hard to grasp. It was easy to split your hand open on them and Batu accidentally did numerous times on the climb up. Some of his fellow slaves didn't make it as well and fell down the side of the plateau to their deaths. It was unfortunate but Batu willed himself to keep going. He wouldn't be like the dead slaves. He refused.

After nearly a day's journey on the climb, they reached the top of the plateau where a giant boulder rested. It towered over all of them and the guards all shouted for the caravan to stop. All of the slaves stared up at the great rock, while the guards circled it and looked around carefully. Batu knew in his gut that this would be it. He was proven right when the guards handed them crude tools for digging and building. Batu immediately got to work with his tool, not wanting to disappoint his spectators. This boulder would be the marker for the grave of the world's greatest leader.

Batu had always feared the Great Khan's personal guard. They were fierce and deadly warriors that could cut down their enemies with ease. And it wasn't just their enemies that they brutalized. He had seen how they would punish slaves firsthand and it usually ended with a dead slave, even for minor offenses. They were impossible to reason with and only answered to the Great Khan and now that he was dead, did they answer to anyone anymore? Or were those violent beasts unrestrained and free to subjugate whoever they wished? Yes, he had always feared them, but now more than ever before.

There was something even scarier about them now. The way they were watching the slaves work on the grave, with blank stares like they barely saw them at all and only saw the work that was being done. They didn't care how many of their slaves collapsed from thirst, hunger, or sheer exhaustion as long as Genghis Khan's resting place was satisfactory for what they wanted it to be.

Batu worked harder than he ever had before, fueled by those tense stares of the guards around him. He refused to falter in front of them, to give the guards any reason to punish him or worse. He could see that his fellow slaves were thinking similar thoughts as they were all working harder than ever to please their masters. They worked tirelessly through the next two nights until the tomb met the guards' desires. They didn't look pleased, but they never usually did. Still, since they didn't look angry either, the workers must have done something right at least.

The slaves—the ones who had survived the work—stepped aside as the late Khan's former guards inspected the burial site. The slaves all waited nervously for a reaction, knowing that some of them could die if any mistakes were found. After what felt like an eternity, the last guard to look over the tomb nodded to his comrades.

Batu let the smallest sigh of relief leave him. This had been one of the stranger tasks that he had been made to do since being enslaved by the Mongols. Once again, though, he had come out of it still breathing. That was all that mattered— making it to the next day. Survival was all he really cared about, no matter the toll it had on his body and on his mind.

Genghis Khan's covered body was carried into the tomb by four of his personal guards. The sight of that made the Great Khan's death even more real for everyone present. The man had traveled across so many lands, seen so many places, and left his mark so he wouldn't be forgotten. But now, he was just like the slaves that had died on the journey—a lifeless corpse. The only difference was that he had a tomb and they never would. That's what it came down to in the end. One's burial site was the only thing that separated them from the other deceased in the world.

The personal guard of the Great Khan all stood in front of them, shoulder to shoulder. None of the slaves expected any compliments or congratulations. They were ready to be ordered to start the long journey back to camp.

Those orders never came.

The guards pulled out their blades and the terror that the slaves already felt was now worse than ever. The expression on the guards faces said it all. The slaves were never going to return to camp. That was never going to be a possibility. This journey was only ever going to end here.

Batu felt his own urine run down his leg as he turned to run away. Some of his fellow slaves tried to do the same but the guards were too quick and far better rested. The slaves never stood a chance as the guards cut down most of them in moments. The few who survived the initial onslaught didn't get very far before being pounced on as well.

Batu tried his best to get away but his legs wouldn't go as fast as he wanted them to. They had carried him too far during this trek and were aching with every step. The rest of his body wouldn't cooperate with him either, not after all of the effort he put into making the Great Khan's tomb. He had no energy left to use.

He didn't understand. They had all done their best. The tomb seemed good enough. Why not let all of them go back to the camp at least? Why waste good workers that had done the deed they were tasked with? Why butcher your own slaves for no apparent reason?

One guard jumped in front of him, blocking his futile attempt to escape. He didn't want to die. He had worked too hard to fall like the rest of the workers had. He wouldn't go down screaming or crying. He would try his best to survive. It was all that mattered.

Batu tried to fight back and threw a punch that hit his enemy directly in the center of his face. The guard stumbled back and initially looked startled by the blow, no doubt surprised that he was facing any sort of resistance at all. The guard even looked slightly impressed, or just a little amused by Batu's tenacity. Unfortunately, the guard responded with a blow of his own, and his came from his blade, not from his fist.

The dagger tore diagonally down across Batu's torso, from shoulder to hip. It was a clean swipe, one that warriors like the guards had probably performed countless times in their lives. Batu could only watch helplessly as his frail body was carved into. He had no shield to block the blade and no clothes to even try to lessen the damage. There was nothing between the sharp edge of metal and his flesh. Batu stared down at the wound in shock, then looked back up to the guard who flashed a thin smile of victory. Batu collapsed onto his side. His red insides pooled around him on the rocks as his life started seeping away, leaving him. He wished he had been given the chance to do more with his life, to leave some sort of lasting legacy like the Great Khan had. No one would remember Batu's name.

As his vision started to grow hazy, he saw the guards stand by Genghis Khan's resting place. They looked calm and resolute with their decision to massacre the slaves. They nodded to one another and Batu just stared, unable to move the rest of his body.

The guards all turned their own daggers on themselves and Batu watched as they all fell. One by one, they pierced their own hearts with their weapons and dropped to the ground alongside the butchered slaves.

Batu's world grew dark, and one lingering thought passed through his brain before the end.

That was it then. That was why this task had been done so quietly. The final step of making a resting place for the Great Khan meant also creating their own. There would be no one left alive who knew where to find the remains of the world conqueror. No one would ever be able to find the tomb of Genghis Khan.

1

A NEW WORLD ORDER

The Order of the Black Sun had changed, just like David Purdue had hoped. They were no longer a shady secret society of megalomaniacs that wanted to desecrate the past to create some warped and insidious future. They were no longer a brutal and hostile group that would kill anyone that got in the way of their plans. They were no longer the villains they had been to Purdue for so long.

Now the Black Sun were cultivators. They were discoverers. They were protectors. They were Purdue's allies, focused on ensuring that the history of the world was safeguarded from being lost or misused. The Order of the Black Sun were the good guys now—at least most of them were.

It was difficult to completely purge the whole order of the toxic members that held onto the way things used to be. Many of the worst had fled the Black Sun the moment Purdue took charge but some of the ones he liked least still remained. They were probably hoping to keep close enough to take charge if Purdue ever accidentally swallowed poison, tripped into a knife, or stepped in front of a firing gun. He had to be careful of them, but none of those lingering threats had acted openly hostile toward him; at least not yet. Their attacks were relegated to verbal ones; nothing more than quiet whispers of insubordination that he could handle.

Since taking control of the secret society, Purdue had spent a lot of energy recruiting fresh faces and more suitable minds, hoping that the new blood would outweigh the less agreeable leftovers of the old order. The people he recruited were passionate optimists who knew their history and wanted to keep it protected, just like he always did.

One of those new recruits, Riley Duda, knocked on Purdue's door and came in with a big smile plastered on her face. She had quickly become one of Purdue's favorites to work with. She was always willing to take on whatever challenge she was presented with, but never stooped to the lows that the old Black Sun operatives would have gone to.

Purdue sat at his desk deep within the Order of the Black Sun's headquarters. He was still getting used to the place and often referred to it as his weekend getaway. His actual home was back in Scotland and had been rebuilt brick by brick thanks to the dying wish of his old butler, Charles. He was thankful for that, otherwise he would be stuck in this place all of the time.

Riley approached and sat at the seat across the table, throwing her legs up onto the desk casually like she always did. Some people might have found it rude but Purdue thought it was actually a very charming aspect to her. Riley was a mostly carefree individual, and the only thing she seemed to really worry about was the artifacts that she helped find. Otherwise, most things just made her laugh—even the dangerous things.

"You look excited as ever," Purdue said with a smirk. "You just in a good mood or do you have something for me today? Something good, aye?"

"Aye! A wee bit of good news, lassie." Riley liked to mock Purdue's accent. It was another thing that probably should have been rude but instead was charming when it came from her. Being from the United States, Riley's only exposure to Scottish accents was from movies and TV; horrible ones like Mel Gibson from Braveheart. She was well aware of how terrible it was and made sure to lay it on thick for Purdue. She liked to make it sound as stereotypical as possible. "Bagpipes in the loch, aye!"

Purdue smiled and waited patiently for her to end her performance. Another good thing about Riley Duda was that she knew not to push a joke too far or drag it out for too long. She'd try and get a smile or two from someone and then get down to business.

"I was just dropping off my latest find in the deep vaults...and let me tell you...it was a good one!"

The deep vaults were one of the best assets the Order of the Black Sun had at their disposal. An extremely secure room that housed all of the relics that the order had collected, along with the artifacts that they had previously stolen from Purdue before he took control. Now, that vast collection was under his protection, it was hard to imagine anyone being able to take those items from the deep vaults. They were much safer there than his items had been when they were stored in the basement of his home.

"Even Elijah was impressed...and that's saying something," Riley said, beating around the bush to build up the suspense as much as possible. She was a rather theatrical person but it was in a good way. "I found an old bow that dates back to the Mongolian empire, one of the ones that dominated everyone else back then..."

Purdue had heard about the importance of bows and arrows to the Mongolian conquest. "They could fire them from horseback with ease, aye. No one else in Asia at the time could compete with that. That's a nice find."

It really was a good find, but hardly anything to look so enthused about. There had to be more, and based on Riley looking at him with baited breath, there definitely was.

"It just got me thinking about the Mongols and especially about Genghis Khan. He's one of the most influential and important figures in history but...no one knows where the hell he was buried."

That was true. There were all kinds of theories about the burial site's location but none of them had been proven true. Those theories alone were fascinating to learn, and Purdue had read all about them on a rainy Sunday afternoon years ago. Many of those theories he learned about came rushing back to him.

According to legends, Genghis Khan had requested to be buried in an unmarked grave and some said that tens of thousands of people came to his funeral. However, to avoid anyone knowing where he was buried, Genghis Khan's army then massacred the people who attended the funeral. His army was then killed by Khan's escorts. The escorts took Genghis Khan's body to its resting place that had been built by slaves. They killed the slaves who constructed the tomb and then, in a final act to conceal the location, the last remaining people to know the truth committed suicide. It had been a chain of death to help conceal the tomb, leaving no one left alive who knew anything about its location.

There was far more speculation about it too. Some said a river had been diverted to flow right over where he was buried, making his resting place impossible to reach. Others said that horses trampled all over the ground he was buried in and then trees had been planted to cover it. Purdue could understand wanting your grave to be unmarked but going through all of those measures seemed little excessive—but a world conqueror and his forces probably didn't care about excess.

Some guessed that he was buried somewhere in Mongolia, and that he might even be buried somewhere near his birthplace in the Khentii Aimag, but those were just guesses. There was a Genghis Khan Mausoleum that had been constructed but it was nothing more than a temple to memorialize him. There was no body entombed there.

Then there was the Ikh Khorig, called the Great Taboo, in Mongolia that many believed and recognized as the conquerors burial site. For centuries it was guarded and trespassing was punishable by death. That certainly made it seem like a suspicious possibility but in the thirty years, it had been opened up and archaeologists were allowed to examine the area. They hadn't found anything that even hinted that it was his real resting place.

Purdue had sometimes thought about looking for the tomb himself but there was just so little to actually go on. All of those stories and legends were severely lacking in any real evidence, any clues that he could latch onto to help him in his search.

Now Riley was barking up that same tree, and he was going to have to break it to her that the tomb of Genghis Khan wasn't exactly going to be easy to find. He loved her optimism and her enthusiasm it was unlikely that they would have enough information to find the tomb or the remains of such an important person.

"There were markings on the bow," she said abruptly, like she could see that he was about to discourage her. "Old scribe that I didn't recognize. When Elijah looked it over, he couldn't fully translate it but the word tomb was definitely on there."

That was interesting, but Purdue really didn't want her to get too excited about so little.

"There are all kinds of stories..." Purdue said. "And people have been looking for a very, very long time..."

Before he could finish letting her down, Riley interrupted. "But have we ever looked? Has the Order of the Black Sun ever actually tried to find it ourselves?"

Purdue didn't know the answer to that. The Black Sun had gone on all kinds of missions in search of things that could help them spread their influence in the world. It was possible but he somewhat doubted that they would care about the tomb of an old conqueror like Genghis Khan. They only would have looked if there was something there that they could benefit from. A long lost skeleton probably hadn't been very valuable to the old order.

Still, the question piqued his interest, and stopped him from completely shutting her down.

"I'll look into it," Purdue said. There may not be any sort of holy weapons or anything like that at the burial site, but the remains of a man as legendary as Genghis Khan were extremely valuable in their own right. Finding a long lost tomb like that could be just the kind of big expedition that the needed to truly bring this new Order of the Black Sun together.

Riley flashed a wide Cheshire grin. "So we're going to try and find the tomb then?"

She looked like an excited little girl who couldn't wait to play a game. Purdue didn't want to completely shatter all of her hopes and dreams.

"I'll give it some thought."

And he already was giving it plenty of thought.

Purdue strolled through the Black Sun compound's halls, passing by many of the order's members. Some greeted him with waves, nods, and good mornings. Others turned away, looking at him with narrow eyes and mumbled words under their breaths. He was used to the mixed reception at that point. He was just glad that he at least had some supporters. Unfortunately, most of the actual dangerous individuals in the order now weren't part of his fan club.

He came to the massive metal doors that led to the deep vault. He hadn't tested it, but Purdue imagined that even a nuclear explosion wouldn't put a dent in those doors. The only way in was with the proper authentication. Purdue put his hand up to the screen as it scanned his palm. He had only been created in the system for a little while and was thankful for it. Otherwise he would never be able to get those doors open. After punching in a few more passcodes, the colossal entrance slowly started to pry apart, revealing an enormous room behind the doors.

Purdue walked into the chamber. Since taking over the Black Sun, he had reorganized the deep vault a bit. Most of the relics he had collected and had since recovered were on display in fortified glass cases, just so he could look them over when he was in a nostalgic mood. They all contained so many memories of his previous adventures, prior to becoming the leader of this secret society. The rest of the artifacts were kept in a pit of well-organized storage, the actual deep vault.

As he walked past some of his favorite trinkets from his travels, he saw a glass cage that had a curtain draped all around it. That was where he had imprisoned the Order of the Black Sun's previous leader, the psychotic Julian

Corvus. That monster of a man had been accidentally given immortality and keeping him caged with all of the other rarities was the best thing Purdue could think of to be rid of Julian. Julian' immortality would keep him from starving or dehydrating in there. That heart of his would keep on ticking until the end of time. That man had taken everything from him; trapping him a small little cage for eternity might have been cruel but Purdue couldn't help feel that it wasn't quite cruel enough. Julian Corvus deserved everything that had come to him. Purdue hadn't spoken to Julian since he first put in him that cage but he hoped that lunatic was suffering.

Purdue came to a large table with all kinds of measuring tools and notebooks sprawled across it. Two people sat on the other side, looking over a few artifacts in front of them. They were hard at work studying the relics and preparing to store them safely away.

One of Purdue's closest friends and colleagues, Dr. Nina Gould looked up from her work and smiled at him as he approached. The two had been through a lot together and each suffered at the hands of the Order of the Black Sun. He knew that she was just as happy as he was to not have to worry about the order being a threat anymore. They had taken one of the most dangerous organizations in the world and turned it into a good thing.

The man beside her pushed his glasses up the

bridge of his nose but didn't look up at Purdue. He was far too focused on the barnacle encrusted cutlass in front of him. Elijah Dane wasn't a very sociable man but, as the Black Sun's curator, he didn't need to be. He was more than content to just dust off an analyze old artifacts that were brought to him by his fellow members. The preservation and safety of the priceless items was his responsibility and he took it extremely seriously.

"Hard at work, aye?"

"Clearly," Elijah said dryly, still fixated on the old sword in his hand. Elijah probably didn't mean to come off as being so aloof; it was just his natural state of being. "I didn't expect to see you."

Purdue held in the urge to tell him that he still hadn't technically seen him, since he hadn't looked up but stopped himself from being too snarky. Nina held in a laugh and looked like she knew exactly was Purdue was thinking. She had been so much happier than Purdue was used to.

"I hear Riley came to you this morning with a rather old bow," Purdue said.

"She did," Elijah said with very little interest. "Mongolian recurve bow. Thirteenth century. Quite aged but an impressive find."

"That's the one," Purdue said with a wink, but that wink never reached Elijah's distracted gaze. "Might I see it?"

"You may not," Elijah said firmly and was still looking over the cutlass in front of him. "Not until you have at least washed your hands thoroughly. And put some gloves--"

"Oh please," Nina said with a hard roll of her eyes. She reached around behind the table and pulled out the old bow, placing it in front of her and presenting it to Purdue. "This is it."

Purdue looked over the wooden recurve bow curiously. It was smaller than most bows but it made sense given it was meant to be used effectively on horseback. It didn't need to be tall as its wielder like a longbow, ready to unleash an arrow from a great distance. It just needed to be maneuverable and easy to fire from atop a mount. With bows like that, Genghis Khan and the Mongols had completely decimated their enemies.

It was worn and withered like Purdue expected and as he ran his index finger along the length of it, he found the engraved markings that Riley had mentioned.

"Riley told me about the writing on this bow. Said you found something that might mean tomb."

"I did," Elijah said with a hint of pride. "But it'll take much more observation before I can know for certain."

"Well that got Riley talking about the tomb of Genghis Khan."

That was enough to finally catch Elijah's attention. His eyes flicked upward and he peered at Purdue curiously. With his index finger, he straightened his glasses and shook his head.

"No one has ever found it."

"I'm well aware," Purdue said with a slight laugh. "But you should have heard Riley. She was very enthusiastic about the possible connection. She was asking all kinds of questions, and that got me wondering...has the Order of the Black Sun ever tried looking for Genghis Khan's tomb before?"

Elijah's brow furrowed. "I'm not entirely certain. There have been no such expeditions since I've been here...but relatively speaking, I haven't exactly been around for very long..."

"So if they had, it would have been before you were recruited."

"Before I was taken prisoner and convinced to work for them, you mean," Elijah said uncomfortably. Elijah hadn't exactly been offered a job. He'd been the Black Sun's captive until he decided that curating artifacts for them would be a better experience than rotting in a cell. "But yes, it would have been before me."

"Is there a chance that there would be any sort of record of that? Of any attempts to find it before?"

"I can't say for certain but I can try my hand at some of the archives." Elijah didn't look pleased about the distraction but pointed to the shelves of books and paperwork lining the vault room. "Perhaps there will be something there."

"Would you?" Purdue knew the answer already. After all, he was the leader of the order and there were perks to being in charge. If you needed something to get done, then you could subtly make sure it happened.

Elijah shifted the glasses on his face again and gave a curt nod. "Sure."

Purdue picked up the bow and stepped away. "I'm going to take this back to my office so I can give it a look with a new set of eyes."

Elijah didn't look at all comfortable with that. He liked knowing that the relics they collected were safe and that meant safe in the bowels of the deep vault. Purdue cared just as much about protecting their artifacts. He just wanted a chance to examine the old bow on his own. He had spent a long time curating his own discoveries. He was more than capable of researching it further on his own.

"I'll bring it right back," Purdue said with a crooked smile. "And in one piece. It hadn't even been stored in the vault yet, aye? Just one extra step before it's under lock and key."

Elijah bit his lip and looked ready to start throwing punches but he refrained and gave a stiff nod again. He couldn't exactly deny the Order of the Black Sun's leader. And even if he disagreed with him, Purdue was a much better boss than Julian Corvus had been. Purdue could get on his nerves but he wouldn't put a bullet in his head if he failed him.

Purdue took the old bow and started walking back toward the entrance of the vault. Nina caught up and strode beside him, shaking her head. "You didn't have to throw your weight around that much you know. Elijah is good at what he does."

"I know he is," Purdue said. "But you can't trust anyone's eyes more than your own, aye?"

"And what exactly are you hoping to see with those eyes?"

"Something interesting, I hope."

"And you think that the order looked for Genghis Khan's tomb?"

"It's possible. They had their fingers dipped into just about everything. They had a long reach and no limitations or boundaries. Remember how many times those bastards would bump into us? It seemed like no matter where we went in the world, the Order of the Black Sun was there. So I don't see why they wouldn't have gone searching for the tomb. We'll just have to see.

The tomb of Genghis Khan could be the perfect opportunity to bring the new Order of the Black sun together. They needed a common goal that could unite the new recruits and the few remaining holdovers from the old Black Sun. Finding a burial site that people had been searching centuries for might be exactly what they needed.

"I'm sure we'll find it," Nina said.

Purdue looked down the hall at the waiting

faces of so many of the other members of the Black Sun. Some loved and respected him. Others wanted him dead. But this was just part of the growing pains of change, and Genghis Khan's tomb might be exactly the right reprieve from those growing pains.

"I hope so."

2

Purdue locked his office door. One thing he missed about spending more time in his actual home was the solitude. He missed being able to admire his relics by himself, with no disturbances that would interrupt his train of thought. As leader, plenty of people were waiting anxiously to ask him all kinds of questions. He didn't have any time to answer those right now. He needed to focus on the possibilities ahead and that meant learning as much as he could about the tomb—and more importantly, the famous figure whose remains remained undiscovered inside of that tomb.

Genghis Khan was a notorious name in history. He was famous for having a very humble start. Over the course of his life, however, he united the greatest land army the world had ever seen and used his forces to conquer an enormous chunk of the world. He crushed so many of the

Chinese dynasties and conquered a large portion of Asia with relative ease. What he was most notorious for was his complete slaughter of the civilian populations of those places he conquered. His conquest was defined by the sheer amount of bloodletting that took place during his efforts. Despite the violence he committed, Genghis Khan was remembered by history as a great leader and military mind.

Genghis Khan died in 1227 after defeating the Western Xia in China and there was no concrete explanation for his death. There were all kinds of stories but none of them had ever been accepted as the certain truth, and with how difficult it was to keep any sort of records back then, they would probably never know the real explanation. Some said he fell from his horse. Some said he died during a hunting trip. Some said that he just got sick. And others said he fell during a great battle. Purdue hoped it was the latter. Someone as legendary of a warrior and military man as Genghis Khan deserved to fall during battle, not by any sort of other mundane mortal way.

After his death, the Mongol Empire pressed on and ended up conquering even more of the world and setting up vassal states to spread their influence throughout the world. From the view of the modern maps of the world, the Mongol Empire that was launched by Genghis Khan had eventually taken over modern day China, Korea, Central Asia, and many more parts of that section of the world. It was all thanks to Genghis Khan and his efforts early on in combining the Mongolian tribes into a united front. None of would have been possible without him.

Purdue was never overly familiar with Genghis Khan's history but he was practically downloading the information straight into his brain with the amount of reading he was doing. He knew the basics well enough but all of the specifics made the Mongol Empire's first Great Khan even more impressive. The Order of the Black Sun's vast collection of old scrolls, parchments, and journals was astounding and he was still getting used to it. It was handy to have first-hand accounts from centuries prior right at your fingertips to use as you wished. Purdue dove into so many old writings and turned to the writings of Marco Polo, who had visited Asia at the height of the Mongol Empire's reign. Genghis Khan was already dead at the time of Marco Polo's visit but he did have interactions with one of Genghis Khan's grandsons, Kublai Khan, and wrote down the accounts he heard about Genghis Khan's death. According to what he was reading now, Marco Polo heard that the first Great Khan had been killed by a poisoned arrow. According to the long dead Italian writer, Genghis Khan was still revered in those decades after his death as his grandchildren divided up his empire to varying results.

Genghis Khan influenced things long after

his death, almost as much as he had during his very eventful life. It was more than impressive, it was what made him such a legend and what made him remembered eight hundred years after his death. He may have been a violent ruler and a brutal conqueror but it was undeniable that he had made a real name for himself.

Maybe there were even some leadership pointers Purdue could take from the ancient Mongolian. After all, he'd managed to unite warring Mongolian tribes to all follow him against the rest of the world. If only Purdue could unite the Order of the Black Sun in a similar way; to get everyone all on the same page and pursuing the same goal. Genghis Khan was proof that a united force could do far more for the world than a fractured, segmented one. That's what he needed. He needed to bring everyone in the order together; it didn't matter if they were new recruits, the old Julian Corvus loyalists, or any of the stragglers in the middle who weren't sure what they wanted to do. He needed to be like Genghis Khan, and take charge of his forces to go conquer the world—or at least, to protect it. Also, he was going to leave out the part of Genghis Khan's leadership that involved massacring the innocent. That wasn't something Purdue felt he could use for his own betterment, that was for sure.

He was nearly done reading Marco Polo's account when there was a sudden knock on the door. Purdue ignored it at first. Hopefully they would get the hint that it wasn't a good time and save whatever questions they had for later. The wrapping at his door continued, growing louder and more incessant until he couldn't take it anymore. He got up from his seat, cussing under his breath, and then hustled over to the door but didn't open it.

"Now is really not the time," Purdue said through the door. "Even if it's urgent. Even if someone lost their damn limb in the mess hall, come back later, and I will address it, aye?"

"And what if it's what you were looking for?"

He recognized that voice. It was Elijah Dane, who was quite possibly the only person in that moment that Purdue would have opened the door for—so he did. Elijah stood there, and like always, was busy adjusting the glasses on his nose.

"What did you find?" Purdue asked feverishly.

Elijah held up a folder. "It turns out the order did indeed try to find Genghis Khan's tomb before. And as expected, they failed just like everyone else who had ever looked for it. They couldn't find any trace of it. Apparently, out of desperation they even went to his memorial mausoleum in Ejin Horo Qi because they had completely dried out of any good ideas."

"That mausoleum is just for show, though," Purdue said. "There's no actual remains there. There never has been."

"Oh, I'm aware," Elijah said. "And I would have told them as much had I been working here at the time. Instead, they wasted a whole lot of time trying to find anything in that tourist trap. Sure enough, there was nothing. So there's not much to go on with any previous searches either, I'm afraid. We're just going to have to carve our own path if we're going to pursue that legend."

"That's fine with me," Purdue said. "I'd rather not try and repeat the mistakes of the people who came before, aye? One thing I learned from all of this." He tapped the books and scrolls in front of him. "It's amazing how much you can actually bring into your modern life. Lessons, ideas, it's never ending."

"I'm glad you're enjoying the writings," Elijah said but didn't seem all that enthusiastic about it. "Just be sure to return them all to their proper places when you're done..." Elijah walked over to Purdue's desk and snatched a glass of water from it, dumping it out onto the floor. Purdue moved to yell at him but Elijah shook his head. "And I would advise that you don't have water anywhere near those papers. If you had spilled this...that would have been it. All of that history would have been gone."

Purdue wanted to remind Elijah who the leader of the Order of the Black Sun really was but he didn't bother. He understood Elijah's need to be paranoid about all of the items from his collection. If anything happened to them, it would be a huge loss to history, especially for Elijah. He liked everything to be in good condition and neatly placed in a safe location.

"So you are going to go through with this?" Elijah looked like he was trying to make conversation. "Searching for Genghis Khan's grave?"

"Aye," Purdue said. "Something like that would be amazing for the order to find. Especially right now when we need a big win. We need to show all of the new recruits what we are capable of here in the order. And we need to show all of the Julian leftovers that they should get on board if they want to be successful, instead of complaining all day about minor changes that they shouldn't have even noticed."

"They are a bitter bunch, aren't they?"

"Yes," Purdue said. "I'm going to need a team of people I can actually work with to find the tomb. That might not be easy. There are a lot of people who aren't ready for a big assignment like this, and there are others who I would never go anywhere with...that would probably kill me the first chance that they got."

"True," Elijah said. "You'll have to be picky with your choices."

Purdue nodded. "I will be."

He would need a great team to find something that so many other groups had tried for so long to find. He would need it to be perfectly balanced and functioning on all cylinders if he wanted any chance to find the tomb. He thought back to everything he had just been learning about the Mongolian conqueror and one question came to mind when considering who he should choose for his team.

What kind of group would Genghis Khan put together?

3

THE TOMB TEAM

One of the benefits to running the Order of the Black Sun was having many more qualified allies to work with. As much as he loved Nina and Sam, there were some things that they were better at than other things. With the new Black Sun, Purdue had hand-selected skilled individuals to recruit so he could cater to a specific expedition with a suitable team.

For their search for Genghis Khan's tomb, he knew Nina would be helpful. Her vast knowledge of so much history was always an advantage that Purdue preferred to have. She had been a prisoner for so long and now mostly helped curate in the vaults. It would be good for her to stretch her legs and see some sunlight again.

August Williams was a behemoth of a man that had been part of the Black Sun before Purdue became leader. He wasn't a particularly bright man, having clearly only been recruited for his muscle, but had been rather bored since Purdue started changing how things worked. They were doing far less underhanded tactics now so his ability to harm people until they gave the order what they wanted was kind of useless. Purdue's order didn't usually need heavies who would hurt people for information. However, having that extra muscle could always come in handy if they got into a bind. And out of all of the older Black Sun operatives, August hadn't shown Purdue any real disdain compared to the others. If anything, he seemed a little indifferent. Maybe this would be a chance to actually win one of the carryovers to his side.

The rest of the team would be made up of Black Sun operatives that Purdue had recruited. Outside of August and his muscles, he didn't want to risk putting too many of the leftover agents from Julian's Black Sun onto the team—at least not with something potentially extremely valuable like the tomb. He preferred to relegate their tasks to more mundane things that he wouldn't mind losing if they decided to take off. No, he needed people he knew that he could trust and didn't want any of the remaining megalomaniacs to ruin his expedition.

Riley Duda was an obvious choice for the team. Not only had she been the one to find the bow and point out the clue it possessed but she had already proven that she was very successful at finding lost things. She always came back to the compound with something of value. She also brought such a bubbly personality to the fold that it would help give the team some positive energy on what could easily be a futile search. They may need her enthusiasm just as much as her other skills.

Yusuke Sanada was one of the first people that Purdue brought into the Black Sun when he started reinvigorating the order. He had always heard stories about the explorer that traveled all over Asia, uncovering all sorts of pieces of lost history. Purdue had been there himself a few times but not as much as he would have if Yusuke hadn't beaten him to so many of its wonders. Yusuke may not have been world-renowned like Purdue but he was well known among historians. He had earned himself the moniker of the Pacific Preserver. Unlike many of the other new recruits, Yusuke had already firmly established himself in the world. He was just continuing his work, but now what he found would be far better protected under the new Black Sun's supervision.

Lastly, Purdue would be on this assignment personally. He'd spent far too much time back at the compound or at home while the Black Sun's operatives carried out expeditions that he usually would have gone on himself. It was the price he had to pay to lead unfortunately. He didn't get to be on the front lines as much, and he missed it. He missed the thrill of the search and the adventures. He needed to get off the bench and actually lead from the front of the pack rather than stay behind.

Once the team was gathered around a table, Purdue looked them all over with some trepidation. He wasn't used to working with such different people. He had gotten so used to working with at least Nina or Sam Cleave at his side. Sure there were times when he would receive temporary assistance from other people outside of his close colleagues but this was a different feeling all together. These people were essentially his employees and he was their boss. They weren't looking to him as a colleague or associate. To them, he was their leader and was higher than them on the invisible totem pole of life. They weren't on even terms with him and would be looking to him for all kinds of answers and decisions. It was a lot of pressure, and he kind of wished that he was just going to stay behind at the compound like usual and not work with all of them on the front lines.

After some brief, awkward introductions, he got around to the task at hand.

"Our objective sounds simple enough, aye? We are going to find the tomb of Genghis Khan. Unfortunately, people have been trying to do that for over seven hundred years and none of them have even been remotely successful."

"As far as we know," Riley interjected with a wink. "Maybe someone found it but didn't want to announce it to the whole world. Or maybe they didn't even know what they found."

"That could be," Purdue conceded. "But as far as we know, it remains undiscovered and that's how he we have to treat this. We only have a few clues to go off of."

Purdue pulled out the old recurve bow and placed it down in front of him, letting everyone get a good look at it. Riley's face lit up with recognition and pride as she saw it. She seemed pleased that the item she recovered was the catalyst for this entire expedition. Yusuke leaned in and looked very interested by it. August didn't quite share his interest from where he stood behind them. He just folded his burly arms and looked down like had no choice but to look at the old weapon. Nina just gave Purdue a supportive smile as he continued.

"Elijah has spent the last few days making the markings on this bow clear enough to translate and has now given a rough translation that he believes to be accurate." Purdue cleared his throat. "The conqueror rests at the farthest reach, at the end of the red line."

It wasn't exactly a clear message and was instead, far more of a riddle. He would have loved if the engraving said exact coordinates. That would have been incredibly helpful, but alas that was all the maker of it bothered to share with them. Still, having something vague was better than having nothing at all.

"What's that supposed to mean?" August asked bluntly, looking around at everyone like they all knew something he didn't. It must have been hard, knowing that his specialty was drawing blood rather than drawing conclusions. "It's a bunch of nonsense."

"The farthest reach..." Yusuke said to himself, rubbing his chin thoughtfully. "The farthest reach."

"Is this the only clue?" Nina asked. "I thought you said clues...plural."

"I did," Purdue said. "There is one more. Elijah did some digging and found that the Order of the Black Sun has searched for Genghis Khan's tomb before."

Purdue pulled out the file folder that Elijah had handed him earlier and plopped it down beside the bow. Nina took the folder and started rifling through the files, looking them all over carefully. It wasn't a large group of files, as the expedition hadn't been long and had borne them very little success.

"It was a failed mission that they went on before. They had very little information to go off of so spent most of their time just wandering aimlessly around Mongolia and the rest of Asia after looking in all of the most obvious places. They never put in much effort, those lazy bastards." Purdue glanced at August who still had his arms folded. "No offense. I'm sure some of the names in that folder might have been friends of yours."

"So that's not much of a clue," Riley said, having started looking over the files herself. "It just rules out a couple of places, but even then, the older Black Sun members might just not have looked hard enough in those places. So really all we have to go on..." She beamed with pride. "...is the bow I found."

"Which is not much," Yusuke said and repeated the phrase aloud. "The conqueror rests at the farthest reach. The farthest reach of what?"

"I'm not sure," Purdue admitted.

"So where do we start? It's not exactly pointing us in a specific direction."

Purdue had given that some thought as well. They could try and deduce the riddle on the bow but they might not get very far or end up in a completely different part of the world than they should be. The safest bet to start, was to check the places that others already thought were high possibilities for Genghis Khan to have been buried.

"Most of the stories and legends agree that he was most likely buried home in Mongolia. So I think we should start the search there, and then see what happens after that."

"That seems like a leap of faith," Riley said.

"It's more than we've had in some of our other searches," Nina said and smiled at Purdue. "We usually end up finding a way to get what we need in the end."

"I've been to Mongolia many, many times," Yusuke said. "I never formally looked for the tomb, at least not anything official, but I had gone on a few day trips just to see if I could find any clue at all. There was nothing. But, with all of you this time, perhaps you will see something that I did not."

"I hope so," Purdue said. "I really want—no I need this one to be a success." Purdue scanned the room again and nodded. "I just wanted to thank all of you for accepting this assignment. I know some of you are still pretty new to all of this..." He nodded to Yusuke and Riley. "And I know others have some experience but aren't too familiar with the way I work..." He offered a small smile to August who just looked disinterested in return. "And then are some who are just sick of me at this point..." He turned to Nina who was just nodding. "But I really appreciate all of you for putting your best foot forward to try and help me find this tomb. Khan died in 1227. That's nearly eight hundred years ago. Eight centuries of people failing to find his remains. An important person like him shouldn't be missing from the world. We should at least know where his grave site is. So thank you for coming along on this adventure with me. I hope I don't let you down."

He was feeling hopeful and he hoped that his

hopefulness wasn't completely misplaced. This team seemed solid. Sure he would have loved to be working with Sam Cleave or even call in someone like occult specialist Jean-Luc Gerard from New Orleans—people he was familiar with —but this was better for growth. He had read something once in one of those nonsense self-help books that talked about how life begins once you're outside of your comfort zone. He didn't know if he believed that but he was open to giving it a shot.

"Pack up your things as best as you can," Purdue said. "We leave tomorrow. Let's go find Genghis Khan."

4

TURBULENT SKIES

It was a long flight to Mongolia and Purdue spent most of it talking with Yusuke. The two of them had strikingly similar lives. Like Purdue, Yusuke had a vast fortune and his many adventures across Asia had mostly been his attempts to satiate his love of history and to curb his boredom. That was very much how Purdue started out. When you had so much wealth and could go anywhere at any time, it just gave you something actually interesting and exciting to do.

The conversation grew quieter as the others started to fall asleep around them. Yusuke leaned in but glanced at a seat behind him where August's hulking body filled one of the chairs.

"Do you think we can trust him?"

Purdue followed Yusuke's gaze to August. He actually wasn't sure how to answer that question. After all, he didn't entirely trust anyone who had been from the previous incarnation of the order.

It was impossible to know how many of them were actually loyal and how many of them weren't just waiting for the right time to restore things to how they used to be. For all he knew, August could just be waiting for the right moment to push Purdue off a cliff. It wouldn't take much effort. There was no way Purdue could fight against someone that much larger and stronger than himself.

"Aye," Purdue finally said, half-lying. "Right now, we've all got ourselves a common goal. August is a big scary lad, I'll give him that, but we may all have to watch each other's backs. August could break my back with his bare hands, aye, but he could do that to any mutual enemies we come across to, understand?"

Yusuke nodded but still looked back at August with some unease. "Everyone talks about how the Order of the Black Sun used to be full of killers, and criminals, and monsters. Is he one of those monsters?"

"He might be," Purdue said. "I'm not entirely sure. We can hope not, aye?"

"But that is how it was, yes? The Black Sun used to hurt a lot of people."

"They did," Purdue said. "Before I took over, the order was willing to go to whatever lengths they needed to if it meant getting what they wanted. Those lengths sometimes included murderer and all kinds of horrible shit. It wasn't a great team to be a part of. As you've been able to see, things aren't entirely like that anymore. I've taken measures to change all of that. And I've recruited people like you and Riley, who aren't here to hurt people. You're here because of the history. August was part of that more violent Black Sun, and I think he was indeed recruited because he could hurt people. I'll say this, he wouldn't have been someone I brought on board. But, I have had to adapt and deal with some of the people that were from the previous version of the order. If August wants to be part of my new Black Sun, then he'll have to adapt too."

"And if he does not?"

"Then we'll see what happens," Purdue said. "But who knows? Maybe he'll surprise us. The Order of the Black Sun that he first joined is gone. He will have to come to terms with that. This expedition might be his best chance to do that. And when he smashes someone to bits help us, we might be glad someone like him is on our side."

Nina wasn't asleep yet. She was staring out the window, deep in thought. Purdue took a seat next to her and gave her a little one-armed hug.

"Having trouble sleeping?"

"Is it that obvious?" Nina said with a small smile. Her eyes flickered over to August's direction and that little smile faltered. "Do you really think it was a good idea to bring him along?"

Purdue laughed, almost a little too loud.

"Everyone keeps asking me that. If I didn't think it was a good idea, then I wouldn't have assigned him to this expedition. We might need some extra muscle, so I brought some extra muscle."

"Sure," Nina said but didn't look very pleased. "I just don't want it to bite us in the ass in the end, that's all. He was one of them, Purdue."

"I know he was."

"I don't think you realize..." Nina stopped and looked back out the window, averting her eyes from Purdue. "He was one of the guards. When I was Julian's prisoner, that big bastard was constantly patrolling the corridors, making sure I didn't escape. Day after day, he made sure that I didn't escape."

"I'm sure he had orders..."

"I don't care if he had orders. I saw him almost every day from my cell. He'd bring me those scraps of food they would give me so I wouldn't starve. He'd stand there, looking down at me and drop those crumbs in between the bars."

"I know it has to be hard," Purdue said, feeling a little guilty. "But all of this...it's a transitional mess, aye? We just have to keep a clear head. Elijah was one of them too, remember--"

"August isn't like Elijah," Nina spat, trying to refrain from yelling. "Elijah helped me. It took a while, but he came around and helped me escape from that horrible place. He realized he was on the wrong side and decided to help all of us. August never had that realization. August spent the whole time lumbering around, making sure I stayed put in my cell. He's only working with us because he feels he has too. He didn't come to our side voluntarily. You really think if anything happens to you, that he'll protect you?"

"I'm not sure."

"And that doesn't scare you?" Nina looked so nervous. "It should, David. Listen to me. I get that you want to make some of the old Black Sun bastards feel included...you feel obligated to include them and maybe that will help break some of the tension, but if it means putting yourself and the rest of us in danger..." Nina took a breath. "I just think we should all be able to trust each other on trips like this. That's the order that I thought we were making. A trustworthy one."

"I'm doing the best I can, Nina," Purdue said bluntly. "And I know...trust me, it does scare me." Purdue looked over at August. "But maybe I should diffuse the situation, aye? Make it so there's no chance of a detonation to begin with."

"And how exactly do you plan to do that?"

Purdue smiled. "With a nice civil conversation, of course. I'm a very persuasive man."

PURDUE TAPPED August on the shoulder and the big man opened his beady eyes. He looked up at Purdue with some annoyance. Maybe waking him up from his nice nap wasn't the best idea but Purdue wanted to be able to speak to him while most of the people aboard the plane were asleep. It was a bit of an awkward situation, and it would continue to be if he couldn't get everyone on the same page.

"Anyone sitting here?" Purdue asked, pointing to the empty seat and obviously knowing the answer. He moved to take the vacant spot for himself but one of August's massive arms got in his path.

"There is, actually," August said.

Purdue managed an uncomfortable chuckle. "Who?"

August didn't answer. He just put his hand down on the seat beside him. He obviously wasn't looking for company. Purdue decided not to sit, as he didn't want to be throttled by one of August's giant arms. So Purdue stood over him, leaning down, but kept a safe enough distance to not be punched.

"Just wanted to have a chat, aye? Just to make see where everyone's head space was at before the actual search."

"My head space?" August growled, folding his arms. "My head space was in the middle of a very good dream before you showed up. What do you really want? Come to check on me? Make a deal where you and I can work together without any problems, is that it?"

"Is that too much to ask?" Purdue said with another nervous laugh. "I'm sure I'm not your favorite person. Did you like the way things were running before...or are some of the changes I've made working out for you...?"

"I was very content, is that what you want to hear? You're scared of me, aren't you?" August glanced past him at the others in their seats, all doing their best to rest on the plane. "They all are. You're all scared of what I'll do. You think I'll blow this whole plane up with you all aboard? Or maybe you think I'll murder you all in your sleep, is that right? I'll tear all of your heads off with my bear hands and then bring them to Julian on a plate before I let him out?"

He wasn't exactly wrong. They all worried that August's loyalty to the old way the Black Sun did things would outweigh how helpful he would be to the team.

"You all think just because I was part of Julian's order that I'm like him. You do realize that there were a whole lot of people in the order that couldn't stand that guy, right? He was crazy. Everyone knew it. Just no one had the balls to do anything about it. Everyone just kept their head low and wanted to wait for things to blow over. If I wanted to kill you, Purdue, I would have knocked your head clean off your shoulders the second you came into the compound."

That was a relief to hear—at least the part about not wanting to kill him and thinking Julian was crazy. Purdue could have done without the mental image of having his skull slapped off by one of August's massive hands.

"Did I hurt people for the Black Sun? Yes. That was my job and I had quite a bit of fun doing it, but I had limits. Julian Corvus never did. Do I wish that you would allow for us to be a bit more forceful with our missions? Of course, but I get it. You don't like spilling blood, getting your hands dirty. I get that...but sometimes that's the most effective way to get things done."

"Not in this order. Not anymore."

"I know," August let out a deep chuckle. "But you might have to, at some point, so it's a good thing you brought me along. If it comes down to it, and we need to do something that you don't have the stomach for, I'll get it done. That might make this whole trip worth it, really...but if you and the others are scared I'm going to stab you in the back...don't be."

Another relief to hear.

"If I was going to turn on you, Purdue, I wouldn't stab you in the back. I'd look you right in the eyes before I snuffed you out. I would give you that much respect before the end."

That wasn't exactly reassuring anymore, but Purdue would take what he could get. At least if August would only come at him from the front, then that would give him ample enough time to at least try to be able to defend himself.

"Why did you join the Black Sun, might I ask? You're obviously not all that passionate about the history or the artifacts. Was it just because Julian offered you a chance to crack those knuckles, aye?"

"It was in a way, yes," August said, cracking his knuckles for emphasis. "He said I would get to travel the world, see some of the most amazing things that Earth had to offer, and every so often I would get to beat someone bloody. Sounded like a good time to me. Far better than my previous jobs. Bouncing people from clubs got tiring. Working security got tiring. It was all just..."

"Tiring?"

"Tiring, yes. There was nothing more to any of them. Just simple muscle work. At least with the Order of the Black Sun, there was something bigger going on. I wasn't just getting tough with people for the sake of it anymore. It meant something."

Purdue understood that. Everyone wanted to have a real purpose. They want their actions to actually be contributing to something. Even a big, tough guy like August needed to feel like he belonged to something larger than himself. Hopefully, that was enough still, even though he was going to be dialing back his chances of brutality.

"Be honest with me now...what do the rest of

the old Black Sun guard have to say about me being in charge now?"

August shifted his big body uncomfortably. "They aren't exactly fans."

Purdue laughed. "And that's not exactly a surprise. Think any of them would betray me if given the chance?"

"Probably."

"Brilliant...and what about you?"

"I don't think so...probably only if I got bored."

"Thanks for the reassurance, big guy."

Purdue got up and returned to his original seat, happy that his talk with August had gone better than expected. Part of him was prepared for a hulking figure like August to get mad and try to take it out on Purdue. Luckily, August proved to be much more reasonable than Purdue ever expected him to be.

Riley suddenly hopped into the seat behind him, smiling and chewing bubble gum. She always had so much bubbly energy and was always fascinated by just about everything. It must have been amazing to see the world through her eyes. Things must have seemed so much less serious and bleak, and so much brighter. She was like a little girl trapped inside the body of a young woman but her childish quirks didn't take away from just how intelligent she was. All of her test scores that Purdue was able to acquire had impressed her, and she already regaled him with some of her more outlandish theories about events in the world.

Riley was something of a conspiracy buff and she was very proud of it. She loved talking about aliens, Sasquatch, and all manner of tall tales that most people wrote off. The only time he didn't see Riley smiling was when she was trying her hardest to prove to someone that those conspiracies had actual factual evidence behind them. She could go on for hours about the Abominable Snowman or things of that nature. Even the little things, like tissues being designed to make someone sneeze more or telephones all being tapped by every government in the world. It was fascinating and ridiculous to listen to.

"How are things?" she asked him, blowing a big pink bubble.

"Things are going more smoothly than I was thinking they would go. So aye, that's a good thing. You might not have even noticed it given how new you are, but there is some animosity between some of our members...with each other and with me."

"Oh, I noticed," Riley said happily. "I've heard all kinds of things. Yeah some people really, really don't like you. But it's just like my mom used to say, you can't please everyone. People are going to hate you for no reason. People are going to love you when you don't deserve it. People like what they like, love what they love, and hate was they things is terrible..."

That was another thing Purdue liked about Riley Duda. She wasn't just hilarious, fun to talk to, or interesting because of her conspiracies. She was young but so incredibly wise for her age. Sometimes, he would forget that in in times like this be reminded that she was someone that shouldn't be judged based on her looks alone.

"That's good advice," Purdue admitted. "I'm not sure if I can follow it to the letter in most situations but I like the sentiment."

"So what's your favorite relic you ever found?"

The question came out of absolute nowhere so Purdue was caught off guard but he should have expected something like that coming from Riley. One second she's as wise as an owl, then the next second she's asking questions that five year old children liked to ask. She was a paradox.

Still, it was a decent question since he felt stumped by it. "I suppose I really liked Excalibur. It's just such a beautiful sword."

For the rest of the flight, those kinds of questions kept being thrown at him in a barrage that he could barely even keep up with.

Who is your favorite person you ever worked with? What is the best place you ever visited anywhere in the world? What did you want to grow up to be when you were a kid? Where do you see yourself in five years? What was the longest lasting romantic relationship you ever had? What season is your favorite? Which member of the old Order of the Black Sun did you hate the most? Which member of

*the new Order of the Black Sun do you like the most?
Which number is strongest?*

The line of questions went on and on and
there was no stopping it. He answered each one
as best as he could and as they went on, the
questions went from mildly interesting and
relevant to his life, to absolute theoretical garbage
but it was still entertaining enough. He both
loved and hated this game. He loved that it was
passing the time in the air but he hated that he
had to get very personal with some of the
questions she asked him.

He tried to slip in some questions of his own
to give to her. After all, he was still trying his best
to get to know her on a personal level. It was only
fair that she had to undergo this trial just like
he did.

Unfortunately he quickly realized that he
already knew most of her answers, as his
recruitment process had a pretty extensive vetting
process. His questions for her didn't last long
anyway, as she would turn them around back
on him.

After dozens upon dozens of hypothetical
questions from Riley, he saw the lights above the
seats let the passengers know to buckle up as the
flight was going to start into a descent.

The plane landed in Mongolia and as
everyone disembarked, Purdue looked at all of
his teammates with some hope. He was among
some incredibly talented individuals who shared

his enthusiasm for the work. August was an exception but he just kept hoping that the behemoth would shock all of them. All he could do was keep wishing that August wouldn't do anything that would stab them all in the back.

Whatever happened, this was the new united Order of the Black Sun's trial by fire.

5

THE GRUDGES THAT NEVER HEAL

Galen Fitzgerald was working on his next autobiography, the sequel to his original book: "Guns, Glaives, and Guinness: The Many Adventures of Galen Fitzgerald". He would chronicle all of the journeys he had been on since his first book; there were many exciting ones to touch on. He had been through quite a lot in recent days, mostly revolving around that bastard David Purdue and his battles with the Order of the Black Sun. Galen had even joined that secret society, hoping to have strong allies of his own to bring down Davy and make a name for himself, but as usual, David Purdue liked making his life difficult and refused to go down. From what Galen had heard, Davy had even become the Black Sun's new leader somehow. That was disgusting thought. He almost felt like throwing up any time he even considered it.

That son of a bitch, Davy Purdue just had to have everything, didn't he? It was just take, take, take, and more take with a man like that. But Galen wouldn't let him have it all. He had made sure of that by taking the artifact that they originally fought over—the Spear of Destiny. Galen had absconded with that holy spear when had the chance. He may have lost his membership with the Order of the Black Sun but he didn't leave completely empty-handed.

Now he just had to figured out what he was going to do next, and working on what would assuredly be another good book was an effective use of time until he figured it out.

Part of him was glad that the Black Sun had fallen and been reorganized. He had planned to work his way up and then make some changes of his own. It was just frustrating that it was Davy who had taken that away from him. Purdue and his new order hadn't come for the Spear of Destiny yet, but he was sure that they would. Davy couldn't let him have it. His ego wouldn't stand for it despite the fact that Galen was the one who told Purdue about the spear in the first place—something he conveniently seemed to be forgotten. The holy lance was rightfully his.

Oniel walked into the room as quietly as ever and sat across from Galen silently, though his gaze made it obvious there was something important on his mind. He couldn't verbally express it, given that his tongue had been ripped out by a former boss, back when Oniel was one of the deadliest men in Jamaica. He and Galen had become close allies during their brief stint with the Order of the Black Sun, having a shared dislike for David Purdue. Even after fleeing the order, the pair remained aligned and both hoped that they would be the ones to finally kill Purdue once and for all.

Oniel was a tall and lanky individual. Even sitting, he seemed to tower over Galen. He had those blank eyes that were impossible to see any real emotion in besides contempt. They would be terrifying to most people but Galen knew that those murderous leers weren't meant for him.

Oniel scribbled on a note pad and then tore a page out, handing it to Galen. It had become Oniel's preferred method of communicating. He always kept a note pad and pen on him to make things easier in their conversations. It barely helped though; between his atrocious handwriting and nonexistent grammar, his messages were nearly impossible to understand. Galen could do with some sort of code to decipher them, but alas, he only had his eyes.

Galen read the scribbles as best as he could, though it took a few moments, and finally figured out what it said.

Purdue and Black Sun
New Goal
Genghis Khan Buried.

So that was it then. Davy and his new friends

were searching for the tomb of Genghis Khan. That was a fruitless endeavor. Galen had looked for that place himself once. It was one of his expeditions that he omitted from his first autobiography. No one would want to read about a failure like that. He had scoured Mongolia but ended up with nothing. Frankly, it was something he didn't like to think about, as it would only make him feel like a failure.

But Davy would probably find it. He always found a way to get all of the glory.

The information on Purdue's plans was accurate; there was no doubt about that. Galen may have left the order but he still had friends who remained part of the Black Sun, and they were more than willing to give him updates on their new leader.

Galen was just waiting for the right time to get some retribution. Some might call it vindictive or petty but Galen didn't care. He wasn't the kind of man that liked to just let go of a grudge, especially a big grudge like this one.

"Thank you, my friend," Galen said with a nod, still staring at the note. "This may be exactly what we need right now."

6

THE WELL-TRAVELED ROAD

The parts of Mongolia near Genghis Khan's birthplace had long been rumored to be the place that his bones were hidden. They had been searched over time and time again by people from all over the world and none of them had any luck. Their excavation of that area wasn't likely to yield any better results but it was the best way to start...to be sure that no one else ever missed anything important. It would be just Purdue's luck to not search there and have that be Khan's resting place the whole time.

Yusuke stood beside him and let out a long exhale.

"I am surprised you never found the tomb, Purdue. You have such a good track record. If anyone was going to find it, I think it would have been you."

"And it still might be," Purdue said with a wink. "I'm honestly more surprised that you never did. You mostly stuck around this part of the world while I was distracted gallivanting all over the place. I would have thought that the famed Purveyor of the Pacific would have found it by now."

"I still might," Yusuke echoed Purdue's jab from a moment earlier, capping it off with a wink.

Yusuke was great and had lived up to his impressive reputation. Not only that, but he and Purdue got along splendidly, to the point where Purdue felt like they were sharing the same brain. He reminded Purdue so much of himself, just a little younger and less jaded...and less wealthy. He was glad to have brought him into the new Order of the Black Sun.

The next day, Yusuke used some of his own connections to enlist the help of one of Mongolia's chief experts on Genghis Khan and his conquest. Shin Wo was happy to help, and was very excited by the prospect of working with famous archaeologists and historians—he was ecstatic to be working with Yusuke most of all. He was very clearly a big, big fan.

Shin didn't speak English very well but Yusuke was happy to translate since he was fluent in most dialects that were spoken in this part of the world—one of the perks of traveling all across Asia on his expeditions.

Purdue listened to Shin Wo addressing him and since he couldn't understand what he was saying, he focused on the man's body language instead. Whatever he was saying about Genghis Khan, it made him move with the giddy excitement of someone much younger than him. He waved gestures through the air as he spoke, gave a reenactment of a battle by wielding an invisible bow, and smiled the whole time.

Despite not understanding the actual words he was saying, Purdue could still hear the cadence, the tone, and the excitement in the man's voice as he explained more and more about the history of Genghis Khan. It said a lot that Shin Wo's enthusiasm for the topic was still so vibrant and palpable despite having to be translated through another language and another man's voice altogether. He spoke with the energy of a master storyteller, getting to each part of the tale at the perfect moment and leaving just enough suspense to make the listener want to get to the next part of the story. When Purdue listened to him, he felt like he was sitting around a campfire or cozily tucked into bed listening to a great audiobook.

Shin went on to talk about so many of Genghis Khan's great deeds. 'Great', however, didn't always necessarily mean anything good. It was more that these great things were important and impactful to the history of the land. Though, there were some actual positives to what Genghis

Khan accomplished besides the conquest and bloodshed. The Great Khan established the Mongolian script, bringing writing to his people. He made sure that there was freedom of religion, something very rare at the time and those freedoms lasted long after his death during the Mongol Empire's existence. It wasn't just all about war with him after all, despite his lofty reputation as nothing more than a violent conqueror. Violence was part of making change to the rest of the world, and maybe that's all it was to Genghis Khan as well. Like most figures who had been dead for centuries, however, it was hard to know for sure. Shin Wo just made it all sound so heroic. He sort of reminded Purdue of a grandfather telling romanticized war stories.

He was obviously very passionate about all of this. If by some miracle, they did end up finding the tomb of Genghis Khan, Purdue wanted Shin Wo to be one of the first people to see it. He'd love to see his reaction.

The excavation wasn't bearing any fruit but Purdue wasn't too surprised. All of the places they had been so far were places that were thoroughly dug up and searched before. They were just giving those places a sweep for safety, to look them over with their own eyes. Purdue never expected to find much there but it was best to be absolutely certain. If Genghis Khan's remains were there, they would have been found by then.

Shin Wo walked up beside him and smiled.

He spoke but Purdue could only look bewildered. He must have looked ridiculously confused. Luckily, Yusuke was close by to share what Shin was saying.

"You know there is not anything here, don't you?" It was like the old man was reading Purdue's mind.

"Aye, I know," Purdue said and his words were repeated to Shin by Yusuke. "I just prefer to be safe instead of sorry. Don't want to miss something without being absolutely sure that we can move on."

Shin spoke again and his message came through Yusuke. "It would be impossible for this to be the right resting place." Yusuke chimed in with his own thoughts. "I searched all over this area one of my attempts. If it were this easy, Khan's bones would have been found a long time ago."

"Aye," Purdue said with a nod. "As for where we should go next, all we have to go off of is that bow that Riley found. Those riddles. The farthest reach at the end of the red line. Mean anything to you, Shin?"

The old man listened as Yusuke translated and then shook his head. Purdue didn't need any translator to know what that meant. That would make things far too easy. He didn't want to rely solely on the writings that were on that old bow but if it was all they had to go on, then that's what they would use.

"We'll give a few final checks here...then we're going to really consider those etchings on the bow."

INTERLUDE - THE PACIFIC PURVEYOR

Yusuke Sanada wanted to be a baseball player when he grew up. He spent so many years in his childhood swinging around baseball bats and catching balls in his gloved hand. He imagined himself playing in front of a crowd of thousands and maybe someday would even travel to the United States and join their professional league. That was how he envisioned his future. He never thought he would be diving into ancient ruins and unearthing priceless relics that most people had never even heard of. It was a far cry from hitting a home run or pitching a perfect game.

His dreams of baseball had started to fade during his teenage years and he found himself paying extra attention when learning about the history of the world from his teachers. Baseball was a great game built with rules and regulations. There was a specific order to events and in how people acted toward one another. There were only so many different things that could happen. Balls would be thrown, bats would be swung, and people would run around in circles, trying to do it more times than their opponents. It was clean and predictable. History was different; it was messy and there weren't any rules that it had to strictly follow, no set way of doing things. There weren't three strikes or foul balls. It was so much more than that.

History won his heart against the great game of baseball. He put down his bat and his glove and picked up textbooks and shovels. His homeland, Japan, had so much rich history that he wanted to uncover, so many hidden secrets that had faded from view with time. Internally, he couldn't completely get rid of his love of the sport as he liked to view his archaeological work as something of a game sometimes. It was that mindset that kept him going.

Within a few years' time, he became very well-known traveling throughout Asia. There were things that he found in places that shocked their own governments. There were things he found that he wished he hadn't. There were things that surprised him but made him all the more grateful that he was doing something he loved.

His passion and his ability to dig up lost treasures drew the attention of the rest of the world. He quickly gained a name for himself on a global scale. They called him all kinds of names.

His favorite was 'the Indiana Jones of the East' as he loved those films but the one that seemed to stick the most was 'the Purveyor of the Pacific'. It was a fine enough name but he really wished the other was used more. He was content playing his game, hitting his personal home runs, and touching home base with a new relic in his hand after the end of a long journey.

Yusuke Sanada hadn't expected to see David Purdue in his home, yet there he was. There had been so many stories going around that even reached Japan. Some said that the billionaire explorer was dead in a tragic accident when his house burned to the ground. Others talked about how Purdue's accounts had all been drained until he didn't have a single cent to his name. Others said that he had been deliberately assassinated by some secret group. There were articles in the news, headlines on papers, and an incredible amount of speculation. Then there was nothing. David Purdue was dead for some time, but now that corpse was greeting him in his own house.

"Mr. Sanada." Purdue approached, offering an open hand. "It's a pleasure to meet you at last."

Yusuke hesitantly accepted the handshake but felt beyond confused. "You are David Purdue."

"Aye, I am."

"I believe you are supposed to be dead."

"That's what everyone has been saying but I'm not the type of man that likes going along with what I'm supposed to do. Truth is, I have had something of a rough period in my life but things seem to be taking a turn for the better as of late. I wasn't dead but I was bloody close to it. Now, though...now I've got more life than ever. You obviously know who I am, and I know who you are too."

Yusuke nodded but still looked uneasy about his visitor.

"I am starting a grand new venture and I would love for someone like you to be a part of it."

"What is it exactly? This new venture of yours..."

"A group. Have you ever heard of the Order of the Black Sun?"

Yusuke shook his head. It was a strange name, whatever it was.

"Good," Purdue said. "I was wondering if they had ever tried to recruit a big name like you before."

"They?"

"It's a long story but the short of it is this...the Order of the Black Sun is a secret society dedicated to looking for all kinds of artifacts and relics strewn about the world. They were run by...well let's just say that they were some real evil bastards. But now, I'm the one calling the shots and I want good people to work with. Given your impressive resume, I thought you would be a good fit. The Order of the Black Sun won't be full of egomaniacs and lunatics this time. It will be staffed by some of the smartest, most skilled, and sane people on the planet that want to see history protected."

Yusuke had always been a solo act. Even on his jobs, he only ever asked for help when there were literally no other possible options left. He wasn't really looking for any kind of group to join since it would feel like he needed the assistance. He didn't.

Then again, baseball was a team sport and there were benefits to having allies to help you in the tough plays. He could have more financial backing, more moral support, and an extra hand or two might be helpful rather than piling everything onto himself. It was a lot of responsibility for one man to have, and a lot of stress to carry. There wasn't anything really wrong with being on a team. It just wasn't something he had really considered before. Maybe it wouldn't be as bad as it seemed like it would be.

"Maybe," Yusuke said. "And you will kill me if I say no?"

"Not at all," Purdue said. "That is not how we do things in the Order of the Black Sun these days. If you had said no to the previous people in charge...yeah you might have ended up in a ditch somewhere with a bullet in your head or strangled to death and dropped in the ocean. But if you say no to me, to us, then you just go about your business. Your life will go just back to the way it always has been I'll still admire the work you do and you will be doing that work without any assistance from us. On the other hand, if you say yes and decide to join up with us, we could give you all kinds of resources to help make your life easier. Believe me, I know from experience how horrible it can be to be trying to find the world's treasures without much help."

That didn't sound so bad—surprising coming from a secret society. Groups like that were usually paranoid about making sure those secret societies remained incredibly top secret. Yusuke had gotten invitations to group before but those were prestigious gatherings meant to just stroke their own egos and flash their own awards to one another. This didn't sound quite like that. The way David Purdue described it was very intriguing. Protecting history was all Yusuke really cared about, and if that was what this group would focus on, then maybe they were the right people to align with.

Yusuke nodded in agreement. "I will see what it is like."

"Brilliant," Purdue said. "It will be great to have someone as respected as you joining the team. If you thought you were having success now, just wait. We're going to be able to salvage so many lost wonders together."

Yusuke liked the sound of that. He would play ball, at least as long as he enjoyed the game.

7

THE MURDEROUS GHOSTS FROM THE PAST

The sun hadn't risen yet but Purdue was already up and ready for the next day of their expedition. It was exhausting but he was pulled awake by the need to make some progress. He walked toward Shin Wo's tent. They were wrapping up their search in this part of Mongolia. Just as he expected, there wasn't anything of value here and there never had been. People before him had scoured this area and people probably still would after, hoping to find some remnant of the Great Khan's life but there was nothing. As they brought this leg of the journey to an end, he wanted to speak with Shin Wo. The man's passion for the subject was infectious and he wanted to bring him along to wherever they headed to next to search. He would be a valuable ally to have when it came finding Genghis Khan's remains. He just had to ask and hoped that Shin Wo would agree to come along. He just needed to make sure that Shin understood what he was asking from him.

"Hey Yusuke!" He called over to Yusuke who looked like he was still barely awake. "Meet me in Shin's tent in like two minutes, aye?"

"Will do," Yusuke yawned.

Purdue entered Shin Wo's tent, calling out to him but there was no response. He peeked more into the tent and saw a mound beneath sheets. The history expert must have needed the rest because he was in a very heavy slumber. That was a bit surprising since Shin Wo had been the first to wake up every morning since he had been helping them. It was weird to even see him sleeping. Purdue had kind of figured that the man just ran on renewable energy and never had to recharge.

"Shin? Time to wake up."

That man was apparently an incredibly deep sleeper. Nothing stirred under the blankets. Not even a single muscle moved. There wasn't even a twitch.

Purdue gently nudged him. He expected some kind of a response; a groan, some muttering, or even a fist to be thrown. There was no reaction, nothing happened at all. Shin Wo remained completely still and silent. Purdue pushed him some more, trying to rustle him awake but no amount of commotion was enough.

The sheets on top of the sleeping man were

sticky. That was when Purdue noticed it. The mattress and blankets were standing with it.

Blood.

It had come from an enormous tear that ran across Shin Wo's neck.

There was no waking up him up from that.

Purdue called out as loud as he could and within seconds, Riley and August hurried into the room. Riley threw her hands over her mouth as she came in. Yusuke followed close behind and he rushed to Shin Wo's side but quickly figured out, just as Purdue had, that it was far too late to help him. August let out a great big sigh and crossed his massive arms.

Purdue hadn't known Shin Wo long and they only shared on word of English but he had become a big part of their excavation efforts and more importantly, was a kind and gentle man. He didn't deserve to go out so bloody. He didn't deserve to be murdered—and by who?

This mission wasn't supposed to be like this. All of the terrible violence and suffering was supposed to stop after Julian Corvus was beaten. It was all supposed to be better once the Order of the Black Sun had changed. None of this made sense. Why kill him? Who killed him?

The image of Shin Wo's bloody corpse started tilting in Purdue's eyes. He was starting to suffer from a bit of nausea being in that tent. This was all just too much to comprehend. This venture had been going so well so far. It hadn't been nearly successful yet but there hadn't been any real bad incidents like he was used to.

"Who could have done this?" Yusuke asked respectfully closing Shin Wo's eyes with his fingers. "Who could have done something this terrible? To him? Why?"

They were all looking at Purdue. That was part of the burden of being the leader and of being in charge. He was supposed to know everything. He was supposed to have all of the answers and be able to make it all make sense for them. But in that moment, he couldn't do that. He had no real answers to make everything seem a little better. An innocent man was dead, probably because he was involved with them. That was on them, whether they liked it or not.

Purdue ignored all of the waiting faces of his new colleagues and stormed out of the tent. If he stayed in that place any longer, he was going to pass out or throw up. It was a truly sickening sight to see someone who was once so serene be killed in such a violent way. It wasn't right. None of it was.

Purdue had to keep moving. He had to hope that the images of that gruesome scene would be swept away in the morning breeze. However, with each step he took, Shin Wo's petrified face refused to leave his mind. All he could see was the blood coming from his slit throat. Whoever had killed him hadn't been playing around. It was brutal and meant to sent a message. And as much as he didn't it want it to be, that message was probably for Purdue.

Purdue felt like throwing up and he bent over, heaving.

This was supposed to be different.

"Top of the morning, Davy. Literally. You're up early, eh?"

Purdue froze, still staring down at the ground where he nearly thrown up. He knew that voice. He knew it very, very well. That Irish accent was one thing, but that smug tone that seemed so sure of itself was unmistakable. And there was only one person in the world who called him that, at least with such pleasure. When he looked up, he knew what he would find—and it was exactly who he expected it to be.

Galen Fitzgerald was standing mere meters from him, leaning on his cane and smiling broadly. That mad Irishman had always caused him problems, especially lately, but he looked particularly ready to aggravate him. Purdue hoped that Galen would find some rock far away and slink under it for the foreseeable future after their last encounter. And now that Purdue was running the Black Sun, Galen had felt the society and left without a word, probably terrified that Purdue would have had complete power of him in that position.

Today was already stressful. Galen's sudden reappearance just made it that much worse. He would have hated seeing him again on a normal day, but after what he'd just seen, it was just another horrible thing to add to the list, and the sun hadn't even fully risen yet.

"Seriously, Galen? How many more times do I have to reject you before you take a hint? I'm not working with you. We're not friends. Stop your whinging and go home."

"I'm not here to be your friend or be on your team, you daft bastard."

"So you came to give me back the Spear of Destiny, aye? How thoughtful of you."

"The Spear was never yours, Davy. I took it fair and square after Julian lost it. So no, I can't say I have any intention of giving it back...because to give something back, someone needs to have something in the first place."

"Funny thing is, Galen, in a roundabout way, that spear is mine. Julian took it for the Order of the Black Sun. It was the order's property and now that I'm leader of that order...well...I'm sure you can fit those pieces together. That spear belongs to the Order of the Black Sun and the Order of the Black Sun now belongs to me. You understand now?"

"Forget the spear, Davy. I'm not giving it to you and you'll never see it again. I'm here to talk about the future. Not the past. I thought we should have a wee bit of a chat before we get into the endgame of our acquaintanceship. Before things start to get messy."

Purdue shook his head. "Things are already mess--"

Purdue froze. In his surprise to see Galen, his mind had gone back to their old grudges, to disagreements they had in the past. It was an automatic response, and had completely clouded his thoughts to the present—to the situation here and now.

"Wait..." Purdue felt that same urge to throw up return to his stomach. "Did you...did you do that?"

Purdue pointed back at his tent and Galen looked past him, following the trail his finger started. He raised a brow and shook his head. "Did what? I don't see a damn thing. You're going to have to be a bit more specific and start explaining things properly--"

Purdue lost his control and rushed forward, grabbing hold of Galen's collar. He put his face right up to his so their noses were practically touching. He sneered, tightening his grip and ready to tear the Irishman apart. He didn't know what kind of game he was playing but he wanted to skip to the end.

"Easy, Davy, easy," Galen said with some nervousness. "Let's at least have a good chat first before we trying beating each other to death. You should know that I'm not stupid enough to come here alone, eh?"

Another familiar face appeared behind Purdue

and put a small knife up to his throat. It was Oniel. He was just like Purdue remembered; tall and lanky with long arms and a shaved head. Those blank eyes of his were hard to miss. Purdue wouldn't forget someone as terrifying as him. What he lacked in words, he made up for with death stares and murderous intent. It had been awhile since he saw him too. He'd nearly forgotten that both Galen and Oniel were working together though. They were an odd pair that had formed out of nothing but a mutual hatred for someone else—Purdue.

Purdue ignored the knife at his neck for the most part, at least the threat of it. But feeling it against his throat did immediately remind him of Shin Wo's corpse. It was making sense now. These bastards were here to try and get back at him, and there weren't kidding around this time. They were dropping bodies. Purdue leaned in closer to Galen, pushing his neck past the blade.

"Shin Wo. You two killed him, aye?"

Galen laughed nervously. "Is that name supposed to mean something to me?"

"The dead man in that tent back there! The one with his throat slit!"

Galen glanced at Oniel who didn't react at all. He was just glaring at Purdue with those hollow eyes of his. Galen looked a little perplexed but his arrogant smirk returned soon enough "It seems like you're having a rough morning, old friend. Let's not make it any rougher. We didn't come here to throw blows just yet. You know me. I'm a rather sporting kind of man. This contest between us will finally end, but I want it to end right. I wanted us to have a chance to speak again before the real fun began."

"Your fun hasn't already begun, you bastard? You killed an innocent man who had nothing to do with you and me. You want to kill someone in their sleep, you should have just gone for me."

Again, Galen looked perplexed and glanced at Oniel. The thought crossed Purdue's mind that Oniel had done the murder of his own volition and not on Galen's orders. He wouldn't put it past Oniel. He was a murderous psychopath who had spent years killing people for the Jamaican crime boss, the Wharf Man. He had no qualms about gutting someone in their bed.

Galen started laughing again. "We'll put an end to this, Davy. Just not quite yet. I see you're looking rather hard for Genghis Khan's tomb. My sources were right about that."

His sources? Purdue had a feeling that Galen still had connections with some of the old Black Sun members but there were only a select few who knew about what they were searching for. The only ones who knew were Elijah and Sam back at the compound, and his team back at the tent. No one else had any idea that Genghis Khan's tomb had anything to do with their assignment.

"We'll let you get back to work then..." Galen snickered, knocking Purdue's hands away from his collar. "Just remember that we're around. You and I will have settle our score very, very soon, Davy."

This was all some sort of stupid scare tactic, nothing more than a threatening warning to try to intimidate him. Galen couldn't just sneak up on him and shoot him in the back of the skull. He needed to be seen and acknowledged. He needed Purdue to know that he was coming for him, and of course he would do it in such a direct way. Galen always liked being the center of attention, and he had just placed him at the very center of Purdue's.

"A phone call would have sufficed," Purdue growled and glanced at Oniel. "And it would have spared an innocent old man from getting his throat ripped out."

Oniel still had the knife up to Purdue's own throat. Purdue wondered if it was the same exact blade he had used hours earlier on Shin Wo. He hoped that at some point, he'd get to take that blade and put it in Oniel's throat. That lunatic should have been put down a while ago. Both of these guys should have but he had been too merciful on his enemies.

Purdue wanted to focus on finding Genghis Khan's tomb. He didn't want to worry about old enemies who he should have already gotten rid of. All of his evil chickens were coming home to roost and he hated that he had ever let them get away with their lives. Of course they would come for him at some point. He should have known better.

"We'll be back, Davy," Galen winked. "When you least expect it. I love surprising you. You should have seen your face when you saw me." Galen let out a high pitched shriek and contorted his face in terror. "You looked ready to shit your pants."

Oniel pressed the knife even harder against Purdue's throat. He wanted to knock the knife away and beat Oniel to death for what he did to Shin Wo but it was too risky. Oniel was a highly skill killer and he could easily end Purdue before he even had a chance to fight back. As angry as he was, Purdue knew that he was in a losing situation. If they weren't looking to end this now, then he should just along with that and live to fight another day.

"Come along, O," Galen said to Oniel. "You'll get your chance soon enough. Trust me. Davy doesn't have much longer to live."

Oniel looked bemused that he had to back down but he listened to Galen and pulled the knife away from Purdue's neck. He stared at him with that empty gaze and Purdue stared straight back at him. Oniel couldn't really speak that well but he had made Purdue a promise once that he was going to be the one to kill him. Purdue hoped not, but he wouldn't be too surprised. After all, he had allowed these ghosts from his past to come back to haunt him, and they were the vengeful kind of spirits.

"Sorry to tell you, Davy, but your reign is going to be rather short."

Galen and Oniel walked away but Oniel did so backwards to ensure that Purdue wouldn't try to follow them. Purdue could just watch as two of the people that hated him most disappeared around the bend.

Shin Wo's death was a terrible way to start the morning, and the return of Galen and Oniel was just making it worse. This was already turning into an awful day, and he didn't think it was likely that it was going to get any better. He somehow felt so much sicker than he already was.

Purdue rushed back to camp and burst into the tent where everyone was still standing around Shin Wo's body in tense conversation. They all looked nervous, some even afraid, and the tension only amplified when Purdue came storming back in. He took Nina by the shoulders, not meaning to look so alarming but couldn't hide his panic and confusion.

"Galen! Galen is here! He's back, Nina. He's here."

Nina shook her head in alarm, trying to calm him down at the same time. "Hold on, hold on, what are you talking about? How would Galen be here? What do you mean?"

"I mean I went for a walk and bumped right into that bastard. Him and Oniel. They're here!"

He pointed in the direction that they had departed in, not that it helped much since he was pointing right at the tent wall. "They were right outside. Right out there."

Nina took hold of Purdue's arms and gently removed them from her shoulders. "Easy, Purdue. Easy. You're not making any sense. You're saying Galen...like the Irish prick that we all hate...is right out there?"

"Yes...I think...I think he...or at least Oniel...I think they killed him..." Purdue glanced at Shin Wo's corpse. "They had a knife to my throat too. I was ready to rip them apart but..."

"You would have died," Nina finished for him, knowing how dangerous those two could be. "Why would they come just to talk to you?"

"You know Galen..."

"Unfortunately," Nina muttered.

"That sick bastard likes to make an entrance." Purdue gestured toward Shin Wo's body and then pointed toward outside the tent. "I guess this was his big entrance. He wanted me to know that he was coming for me, for all of us."

Yusuke and Riley were both listening with some confusion. They had no idea who Galen or Oniel was, as they were before their time with the Black Sun. Purdue must have sounded like he was going crazy with everything he was saying. August, meanwhile, stood tall in the corner of the tent, his big arms crossed. Unlike the other two, he knew Galen and Oniel so he wasn't exactly surprised by a stunt like this.

Purdue's mind was racing, swirling with questions and concerns.

How did Galen find them? What sources was he talking about? Who would have told him about their current search? Who would have turned on Purdue so quickly and sold him out to Galen Fitzgerald?

Purdue turned to August. He didn't really want to jump to conclusions but there were only a few possibilities and only one glaringly obvious one. August was part of the old Order of he Black Sun, just like Galen had been. They might have even worked together during that time. It wasn't like he knew August enough to fully trust him.

"You keeping in touch with your old pals, aye?" Purdue blurted out angrily. He tried to keep calm but his heart was pounding in his chest. He just needed to figure out what the hell was going on and he needed to do it fast, even if it was a messy way to get answers. "Is that it?"

August raised a brow. "What are you talking about?"

Purdue couldn't hold back his anger much longer. "I'm talking about Galen, obviously! You let him know where we were. You sold us out, didn't you?"

August scoffed and shook his head. "You really think I would do that?"

"It makes sense."

"No, it doesn't," August said coldly. "It doesn't make any goddamn sense at all actually and you couldn't be more wrong. I never liked that prick and I definitely wouldn't work with him. Not ever. That's for sure."

"And, what, I'm supposed to just believe that?"

August folded his arms and kept shaking his head. "You can believe whatever you want. It doesn't matter to me."

Purdue glanced at everyone else. They all stood around them, watching it all uncertainly. They were wide-eyed and looked just as nervous as Purdue. Part of him wondered if he was just being paranoid but no...no there wasn't any other explanation. It had to be August. It had to be.

If it wasn't, then who could it even be? He was the most likely suspect. He was part of the Black Sun when Galen was. The others weren't. It was the only thing that made sense. But if they spent too much time arguing among themselves, then they would never find the tomb.

Purdue thought over the other potential suspects that could have been working with Galen but none of them added up as well as August. Nina hated Galen even more than Purdue did, and would never even consider teaming up with him. Plus, she and Purdue had been through far too much together for her to just stab him in the back now. Nina wasn't a real option, as far as he was concerned. There was no chance in hell that she would be turn into a traitor.

Yusuke didn't seem very likely either, but maybe that was just Purdue's bias. They had been getting along so well in the short time that they had been working together. Purdue, Yusuke, and Galen had all been healthy and successful hunters of artifacts—less wealthy and successful in Galen's case—so they had traveled in similar circles. Hypothetically, it was possible that Yusuke and Galen could have met before but why would Yusuke work with the Irishman over the order? There was nothing that Galen could offer that was better than what the Order of the Black Sun had already given Yusuke. His induction meant that he had allies, resources, and support from like-minded individuals. Working with Galen wouldn't get him anything more beneficial than those. Even their personalities seemed so opposed and unlikely to function well together. It was possible, but certainly unlikely.

Then there was Riley Duda. She was someone that Purdue was a little less sure of. He liked her a lot but didn't know her as well as Nina or feel as connected with her as Yusuke. This whole expedition was her idea, though, so why would she work with someone like to Galen to interrupt it and throw a wrench into the mission that she started? That didn't make any sense either.

August was the only one that had a concrete

history with Galen, the only one who might share Galen's grudge against Purdue, and the only one with a motive that seemed remotely sensible. It had to be August. Even if it wasn't, they had to be careful.

"Purdue," August said grimly. "Remember what we talked about on the plane? You remember that? I was serious about everything I said then. Dead serious. That was all the truth. Right now, it's still the truth. I'm on your side."

Purdue reached into his bag and pulled out some rope. "My side...yeah...then you won't mind if we put this around your wrists, aye?"

"Of course I would mind that," August said with gritted teeth. "Anyone would."

"Well tough luck, lad, because that's what we're going to do until we sort all of this out."

August's head was still shaking, just as it had been during the whole conversation. "You can't be serious about this."

"Very serious."

"You really think I would kill Shin? I liked the guy!"

"Well, it's not a huge leap, is it? You have a history with violence. You've probably done plenty of kills like this before."

"Not like this," August said firmly. "I have more respect than to cut someone's throat in their sleep. That's coward shit. When I was enforcing for Julian, I always made sure that my opponent had some sort of fighting chance!

Killing him in his sleep doesn't sound like much of a fighting chance to me. And you are so quick to point fingers and throw around accusations but I remember that Dr. Gould there killed Julian Corvus at one point, right?"

Nina frowned, and Purdue felt a tinge of anger that August even brought that up. Nina had been fighting for her life back then. It was kill or be killing, self-defense, and definitely not murder. The person she killed had also been one of the most cruel men Purdue had ever met, not some old sleeping historian.

August continued. "Sure, Julian was brought back to life by the Spear of Destiny but she still killed him." August looked at the others. "I'm sure we all have at least some blood on our hands. Mine have just been stained a bit more than the rest of yours—more than most peoples' probably. But I would never, ever do this."

"You have some balls to bring up what Nina did. It's entirely different--"

"Purdue..." Nina cut in, putting a hand on his arm. "We don't know for sure..."

Purdue couldn't hold back all of the negativity flowing through his mind. He didn't know what to believe. Galen's ambush had sent this whole expedition into disarray. He should have dealt with that Irishman immediately instead of letting that threat linger. Of course Galen was going to still be a thorn in his side. That's what he had always been. That egotistical little bastard excelled at trying to ruin Purdue's life.

If Purdue had another chance to stop Galen for good, he wouldn't hesitate this time. Galen may not have been as dangerous as Julian Corvus or some of the other enemies over the years but he was much more vindictive than the rest. Galen wouldn't stop until he was standing above everyone else, and they were all complimenting him on his greatness. That kind of pettiness was dangerous, because it would never stop, and wouldn't hesitate to throw some low blows.

Purdue was angry at everything. He was angry at Galen and Oniel for daring to show their faces anywhere near him again. He was angry with August for seemingly and most likely being part of whatever their scheme was. He was even a bit mad at Nina for trying to rein in his wrath. Most of all, he was angry with himself for letting any of this happen. As leader of the Black Sun, he was one of the most powerful men in the world and he couldn't stop one man who barely had anything to do with all of this from dying. Of course he was angry, because nothing in the world was going the way he wanted it to.

"We need to get our heads screwed back on straight," Nina said, looking mostly at Purdue. "We can't let that little shit get into our heads that much. That is what he wants. Galen loves throwing wrenches into things, just to see how much of a problem he can make. That's what this is. He has been obsessed with you for years, Purdue. He just wants your attention."

"Well, then he's got it!" Purdue yelled, pointing at Shin Wo. "We have to stop him."

"Sure but we don't have any idea where he is," Nina argued. "Not a single idea. You know what we have an idea of? Where the tomb of Genghis Khan is. We have the writing on the bow to go off. That's far more than we have for Galen. He could literally be anywhere. He says he's coming for us? Let him. Let him try. We don't need to worry about finding him because he's already going to be coming to us. So let's get back on track and get out work done. If he wants to follow, he can and we will deal with him then just like we have dealt with him every other time that prick has tried to hurt us."

She was making a lot of sense and Purdue ease just a little bit. He still wanted Galen found and dealt with but her plan was probably best way to get to that end. He slowly nodded and she rubbed his arm.

"I know this is a crap hand we've been dealt, but we've survived worse. Galen isn't Julian. We can play him much more easily than we could Julian."

"Okay, we'll let him come to us..." Purdue conceded.

He looked past Nina at August. The big man still looked uncomfortable after the blow out but Purdue wasn't sure if he was playing it up or not.

He might just be trying to look as innocent as possible. No matter what Nina said about sticking together and not let Galen get into our heads, the facts were still the facts. There were very few people who could have or would have helped Galen get to them, and the one that made the most sense was August.

"So am I going to be carted around in handcuffs the rest of the trip?" August asked belligerently. "Or are you going to leave me here? How are we going to do this?"

Purdue was tempted to give a spiteful reply but Nina intercepted before he had the chance. "You will be coming along, August. You're innocent until proven guilty as far as I'm concerned. Things are...this is all complicated but we need all hands on deck with this one."

Purdue wanted to start arguing again. August wasn't exactly an essential part of the team's search. He was meant to just be there for the physical support. There was no reason for him to come if they couldn't rely on him to protect them; they especially had no reason to bring him along if there was a chance he could kill the rest of them in their sleep.

Nina turned to Purdue and gave him a hard stare. "Right?"

She practically impaled his rib cage with her elbow.

Purdue played along, but he wasn't at all pleased. "Right. Innocent until proven guilty."

GALEN THOUGHT his reunion with Purdue went fairly well. Actually, he was surprised by just how upset Davy looked...and some of the things he was saying hadn't made much sense. Something else must have happened with Purdue, because usually he was much more full of himself and wasn't so emotional. Those accusations about ripping some old man's throat out were curious, to say the least. Galen looked to Oniel who sitting across from him. It crossed his mind that maybe Oniel went ahead and did something without letting him know.

"You kill some old man who was with Purdue?"

Oniel shook his head. Oniel was a great many things but he wasn't a liar. He would have told Galen, especially now after confronting Purdue. There was no reason to hide what he did at this point. So there was more going on with Purdue's expedition than there seemed.

Oniel looked down to his note pad and started scribbling down frantically, so hard that Galen thought the paper would rip apart or the pen's tip would snap right off. When he was done, Oniel ripped the paper off of the pad and slammed it in front of Galen.

Why is he still alive?

Galen was only just starting to get used to Oniel's new way of communicating but it was grating on him already. He preferred when Oniel could just shoot him a glance or make some face to let him know how he was feeling. Now he was...a bit too chatty.

"He's still alive because we haven't killed him yet, of course," Galen said facetiously. He didn't need to be questioned by a man who couldn't even speak. Oniel should have realized by now that Galen was in charge of the plans and Oniel's only job was to use his knife well when they needed it. "Obviously, eh? We haven't done the deed."

There was more aggressive note taking and then another slip of paper was placed in front of Galen. Oniel's cold stare was transfixed expectantly on Galen, like he wanted particular answers. Galen looked down at the new piece of paper.

We should have.

Galen understood Oniel's confusion but it wasn't his place to be demanding answers from him.

"No, my friend...we could have. There's a difference. That was not the time or place that we should have killed him. That part is still to come, eh? Trust me."

The next note was written quickly but with even more aggression than the previous two. There was only one word written on it,

NOW.

The three letters were practically carved into

the paper, nearly shredding it completely. Galen read the word, shook his head and looked up at Oniel. "Do they not have patience back where you're from? Did the Wharf Man have no sense of timing? I've been waiting a long time to get back at Davy...a hell of a long time. I'm not going to waste it and ruin it by rushing the whole thing. This needs to be perfect. And I want to get as much victory from it as possible. He and the new Black Sun are looking for Genghis Khan's tomb. Knowing Davy, that bastard going to find that tomb...and when he does...we swoop in...we rip that win away from him. That's when we kill him and his friends...and that's when we take Genghis Khan's remains for ourselves."

Oniel didn't blink. He stared straight at Galen with those hateful, spiteful eyes and Galen just looked back without backing down. Galen had known and hated David Purdue far longer than Oniel. If anyone was going to decide how to end Davy's life, it was going to be him. Oniel's hand was still on the pen and Galen half-expected him to drive that writing utensil into his throat. An experienced killer like him easily could...but then Oniel dropped the pen. He didn't touch his note pad again.

There didn't need to be anymore conversation, the argument was over, but Galen wasn't quite done yet.

"I know you have that itch to kill things...to be honest it's one of the things I like most about you.

It's probably why we're such good friends, you and me, but there's really something you need to work on. You want Purdue dead, so do I...and he will be but we're going to do it properly, eh? You worry me sometimes."

Galen snagged the notepad and pen off the table. At first, Oniel looked livid and ready to murder Galen right then and there for the theft. Losing that note pad must have been like losing his lips or losing his tongue again. He wouldn't be able to make his thoughts known as easily now, but Galen had no intention of keeping the pen and paper. He jotted down a few words and then slid the paper back to Oniel and rolled the pen back to him across the table. Oniel looked at the scribbles and then nodded. Galen's note was brief and to the point:

Be Patient. You have no sense of poetry.

INTERLUDE: THE SMILING GIRL WHO WANTED TO BE REMEMBERED

Riley Duda no longer expected to do anything all that important with her life. She never thought that she had some sort of higher purpose in the future. She never believed that she would ever really many any sort of impact on the world at large, or even leave any real lasting impressions on other people. She didn't expect to ever be remembered like the people through history that she loved reading about. Her name wouldn't be remembered like theirs. She would just be one of the billions upon billions of forgotten names, for people that weren't important enough to even be remembered at all.

Joan of Ark. Anne Boleyn. Amelia Earhart. Cleopatra. Queen Elizabeth. Harriet Tubman.

Those were women that wouldn't be forgotten. They had carved their name into the fabrics of history. Riley would never be among them, no matter how hard she tried. She had even come to accept that. She had grown accustomed to just reading about the exploits of far more influential people. It took something special to do something great and often required being part of something bigger than just yourself; being a voice in something that actually affected the rest of the world.

Riley spent most of her youth trying to make a name for herself. She was always top of the class. She was always involved in all kinds of extracurricular activities and had done an incredible amount of fundraisers and charity work. She had tried to go through life with a thirst for knowledge and tried to make sure she always had a positive outlook. Letting herself think negative thoughts would only inhibit her progress so she pushed through those whenever she could. She wanted to make a difference in any way she could, even if she could only make small changes. She had high hopes but as she entered adulthood, she gained a more realistic perspective and accepted that she wouldn't be one of those names that would be solidified in the history books.

She didn't think that purpose and destiny were something that were meant for her—but then she met David Purdue.

Suddenly, she saw that it might even be possible to actually make a real difference in this world. There was potential to actually be remembered. David Purdue wasn't just a good looking man but an incredibly charming and persuasive one. He presented her with a very convincing pitch that captured her interest and had no chance of letting go of its hold.

According to him, she was being invited to join something called the Order of the Black Sun. It was a weird name but Riley had experience being a part of clubs and organizations. They just usually weren't secret societies. This Order of the Black Sun was apparently trying to find artifacts that had been lost in time and were trying to protect history and the memory of mankind. It all sounded great but Riley spent a good portion of the time wondering why she was even getting the invitation. After the proposal seemed to be winding down, she voiced that very question.

"Why me?"

David Purdue smiled pleasantly. "Because you have potential, Miss Duda. Lots of potential. Tell me, haven't you ever wanted to do something important in your life?"

It was like he could read her mind.

She nodded, and in that moment, began what she hoped would be a life changing adventure. Maybe there was such a thing as purpose, because this really felt like it could be hers. If everything this Scotsman said was true, then she really might be able to join the ranks of all of those remembered names someday.

Riley Duda couldn't stop smiling.

8

THE ONES LEFT BEHIND

Sam Cleave felt a bit left out. He was fine not being assigned to go find the tomb of Genghis Khan; it was just part of how their new version of the Order of the Black Sun was going to be operating. People were going to go certain places based on their experience and helpful qualities to that particular assignment. He didn't have anything in his skill set that would make him particularly useful when looking for Genghis Khan's resting place, so he understood why he was left behind. He tried his best not to take it too personally.

Still, it was a bit strange to see Purdue and Nina leave to go on an adventure without him. The three of them, despite being separated by circumstances sometimes, had worked together for so long and on so many different expeditions. They had traveled all over the world together, faced death countless times, and done very well for themselves even in the face of incredible adversity. They were a pretty great trio of collaborators and they were great friends too. Of course Nina would be a great help in most ventures. She had a vast knowledge of history that would be great to have by your side in most situations. Part of Sam wished that he had something as valuable to bring to the table. All he really had going for him was his skill at getting information as well as his tenacity. That was it.

He wasn't a huge fan of Purdue's decision to repurpose the Order of the Black Sun and had continued to try and get used to the idea, but it was taking a lot of adjustment. The Black Sun had been nothing more than their enemies for so long that it was tough to realize that he was now a fully-fledged member of their ranks. It didn't matter how much the society was changing. It didn't matter that it might be something great at the end of this metamorphosis. For now, it was still in its transitional face, and still at least partially the old Order of the Black Sun that he remembered. He had initially suggested to Purdue that they just let the Black Sun fall apart after they beat Julian; to let it burn to the ground until there was nothing left but Purdue wanted to redirect the power of the Black Sun instead. He didn't want all of their great resources go to waste. Only now, Sam was starting to see Purdue's point but it was still a struggle for him, especially after how much damage Julian Corvus and the old Black Sun had to done to his life.

In times like this, left behind at the Black Sun compound, he had plenty of time to contemplate his new role in life. Some of the faces he passed by in the halls were fresh faced rookies who had no idea how dangerous getting involved in this kind of business could be. The others in the hall were people that had already been with the Black Sun at the time of Julian's defeat. He was pretty sure that he had punched a few of them in the face before during one of his more hostile encounters with the order back in the day. HE hoped that they remembered that and he also liked to think that was why they were keeping a fair distance from him in the compound's corridors. He didn't even remotely consider them allies yet. He couldn't. He still looked over his shoulders here and there, waiting for one of his old enemies to decide to make a move. Some might call it paranoia, but he preferred to be cautious in such a strange situation. Purdue might have been fine letting those old grunts make the jump to their side, but Sam wasn't quite as forgiving.

Sam went into the deep vaults, one of the only places that he actually felt comfortable in at the Black Sun headquarters. That was partially thank to the enormous metal doors that cut him off from the rest of the order when he was inside, and partially due to Elijah Dane, who had already proven that he could be trusted despite having been the Black Sun's curator. He was an awkward and cold, but there was peculiar charm to the man and he could at least hold an interesting conversation.

When he saw Sam enter the room, he pushed his glasses up the ridge of his nose ambivalently. It was the usual greeting that he gave people, nothing overly welcoming but Sam was getting used to Elijah's inept social skills.

"How is it going in here?" Sam asked. He had been visiting Elijah at least once a day, realizing that it was a good way to pass the time while the others were off on their grand adventure to find Genghis Khan. "Given anything interesting lately?"

"Since yesterday?" Elijah asked with a yawn. True enough, there hadn't exactly been a lot of time since they last spoke; probably not enough time to have been presented with anything good to put away in the vaults. "No, Sam. Nothing of note. I've been too busy looking a bit more into Genghis Khan in case Purdue calls again needing more information. They've been a bit stumped of late, I'm afraid."

A very small part of Sam was a little glad that they weren't having a super easy time without him. Maybe they would bring him along next time. Then again, if Purdue and Nina were stuck on something, then it probably was something Sam would even be able to help with.

"Where are they right now?" Sam asked.

"They were in Mongolia but that proved unsuccessful like Purdue knew it would. Now they are on their way to China. Oh...and Galen is after them."

Sam thought he misheard for a second but then the name sunk into his skull.

"Galen!? The hell does he want!?"

Elijah didn't appear very concerned. "What Galen always wants...attention. I was here when he was part of the order, remember? Every single thing he did was for validation from his peers. He would bring me a relic to put away and spend the whole time waiting for me to praise him. I never did. I don't partake in unearned praise, especially if I am expected to give it to dimwitted man-children."

That cold logical way that Elijah had about him sometimes upset people but Elijah enjoyed hearing it in moments like that. Sometimes Elijah seemed so robotic; it was nice to know that there were people that he felt so strongly about, even if that feeling was disdain.

Sam was thinking about Galen now. They should have finished him off back in the Arctic, the last time they saw him when they were in that teleporting Mayan temple. Then he wouldn't still be around to stalk Purdue and the others. That man couldn't get the hint that they didn't want him around. Either that, or he was begging Purdue to let him back into the order.

Whatever that crazy Irishman was after, it couldn't be good.

"You wish you were there, don't you?" Elijah asked, eyeing Sam curiously. "Look at you. You're just a walking, talking ball of anxiety."

"Thanks," Sam said. "I didn't realize that it was that obvious."

"It is."

The deep vaults fell silent for a few minutes as Elijah kept looking through some old scrolls. Sam peered around at the trophies that Purdue liked to put on display, relics that he was especially proud of. The rest of the Order of the Black Sun's vast collection were stored down in the pit underneath the room. He saw the tall curtains blocking the immortal Julian Corvus' cage from view on the other end of the room. The box had a speaker system so he wasn't actually able to hear any discussions out here unless they wanted him to. He was fine with his old enemy being trapped in such a small box. It was what he deserved after what he did.

A ball of anxiety...Elijah hit the bullseye with that assessment. Sam was practically itching to get out and do something. He hated being completely useless thousands of miles away from where his friends could be in danger.

He let out a frustrated groan. "How did this happen? How did we get stuck back here? Why are we the ones that got left behind? We both have proven that we can contribute, haven't we?

Hell, we helped bring down Corvus. Why should we get left in the dust while the others all get to go make a difference?"

Elijah rolled his eyes behind his glasses. "I don't mind at all. I actually prefer it this way. I don't have the stomach for field missions. That one trip up north to that temple was plenty enough for me. I'm content sitting right here, and waiting for all of the others to bring me the spoils of their adventures. I get to see the best part of it, no need for everything else."

"That's right," Sam said with a snicker. "I forgot that you like boring places like this. Some of us need to be out there, making a difference. You wouldn't even get those relics if not for people like that. You know that right?"

"I can't argue that," Elijah conceded. "It's true, but my point still stands. For me, this is certainly the best place for my talents. This is my adventure. You can have yours. And what about yours, Sam? You seem on edge, so what are you going to do about it? Are you planning on racing to China to come to their rescue? Purdue and Dr. Gould chose their team for a reason. It might bother you, but they also chose not to take you for a reason. You should respect your friends' decision, shouldn't you?"

Elijah wasn't wrong—he rarely was. Sam did want to go help Purdue and Nina. He wanted to be the much needed reinforcements that could turn the tide in the eleventh hour to whatever trouble those two got themselves into. But Elijah had a point, as always. Sam should respect Purdue's decision, not only as the leader of the order now but also as a friend. Obviously leaving Sam behind was done for good reason and it was a decision that was made for everyone's benefit. Throwing himself into the mix would complicate things, or maybe even make things worse for everyone involved. He didn't want to be responsible for that.

Sam decided to take a seat across from Elijah and make himself comfortable. He wasn't going to be going anywhere so he might as well get used to hanging around for a bit. Elijah looked pleased with his decision, like he had just disarmed a ticking time bomb. He handed Sam a scroll and a translated version of it.

"Look over these. There might be something important in them. If you notice anything...anything at all, just say so. Even if it's useless."

Even if he wasn't out in the field, Sam could still be helpful to the mission. Maybe he could help from back home, doing the research and acting as the brain to Purdue and Nina's hands. That could be just as important of a job as hiking through treacherous terrain or diving deep into the sea. Before Sam got too caught up in the words he was reading, he looked up at Elijah.

"Did they give a more specific place where they're going?" Elijah looked at him with some

PRESTON WILLIAM CHILD

annoyance, thinking that Sam was contemplating going again, but he wasn't. "I'm just curious. Do we have a more precise idea of where they are."

"They're going to investigate some more over at the location of one of Genghis Khan more well-known triumphs. The Great Wall of China."

9

THE OPTIONS ON THE WALL

The Great Wall of China was recently considered one of the wonders of the world, but the truth was that it always had been one of the world's most impressive wonders. Stretching across twenty-one thousand one hundred ninety-six kilometers, and standing nearly thirty feet tall in some places, it was still to this day a marvel to behold. Especially given when it was built, it was incredibly impressive. Much of it had been renovated and added onto over the centuries but its primary function had always been to protect China from foreign invaders. Among those invaders were the Mongols.

One of Genghis Khan's most infamous accomplishments was breaching through the Great Wall to invade the dynasties of China in the early thirteenth century and swept through

North China with ease. He brought down China on his road toward world domination.

Of course, breaching the Great Wall hadn't been some legendary siege or anything like many would imagine it would have been. Genghis Khan was indeed a great commander but not much advanced tactical prowess was even needed at that time. Genghis Khan and his Mongols simply found the parts of the Great Wall that had been falling apart at that time—and much of the wall had holes in it—and they rode their large amount of mounted cavalry straight through those openings into China. The wall was much more solid now than it had been back in the 1210's.

Purdue had been to the Great Wall of China before, as both part of expeditions and for pure leisure. It was one of the benefits of having so much money over the years and for having the hobby that he did. He found his way all over the world for one reason or another. But, in situations like this, sometimes he looked at a place completely differently based on why he was there. Looking for any clues about Genghis Khan's remains was much different than just trying to take in the sights and walk the length of the wall as a tourist.

"You really think there's anything here?" Nina asked. "I've got to be honest. I'm not convinced. This is one of the most frequently visited places in all of Asia. It's not exactly an ideal place to secretly bury Khan. Even then, it probably wasn't the best place. And with all of the construction that's been done over the centuries, I imagine someone would have stumbled upon his tomb, right?"

"To be honest, I don't expect there to be much, no."

"So this is a waste of time?"

"A waste of time? No. Not exactly. It gives me a little more time to figure out what to do about the problem we have on this team."

Nina followed Purdue's gaze down the top of the wall where August was standing and looking around for any little detail that they might miss, trying to find any clue he could about Khan's burial place. If Purdue was right, then August wouldn't find much no matter how carefully he looked, but that wasn't the point of this stop, not really.

"You mean with August?" Nina asked with a shake of her head. "Purdue I really think you're wrong about him."

"And if I'm not?" Purdue asked, trying to hold back his frustration. "An innocent man is already dead, aye? And if it was August, then that's on me for even allowing him to come along on this trip. I could have picked someone else...someone new or even Sam even. Hell, I could have dragged Elijah out from the deep faults to go on a field mission. None of them would have hurt anyone. But instead I brought along August just in case I needed the extra muscle...but that extra muscle might be the very thing that kills us. It's a bit of a mess and to be honest, I'm a bit on edge, if you couldn't tell."

Nina took a breath and ran a comforting hand against his back. "I know. I know, it's just...there's not enough evidence. Circumstantial things is all we have. Yes, if you're right and he really is working against us from within, then we could be in some serious trouble...and yes Shin Wo's death really would be on our hands...but if you're wrong, you could be condemning someone completely innocent for nothing. He could be an asset. You know he could. That is why you really brought him along. What he lacks in brains, he makes up for in strength and sometimes you need a combination of both on these journeys. Sometimes you, me, and Sam could have used a big strong guy like that watching our backs, couldn't we?"

"There would have been a few situations where they would have been nice, aye."

Nina patted him on the back and walked the other direction to go see if she could see anything. There was only the tiniest chance that anything related to Genghis Khan would still be here so Purdue wasn't expecting much. This was all just a small detour to give him time to think about all of the bad things that had transpired...and August's possible role in them.

Purdue stared out to the lands north of him.

Walls that divided people were interesting things and usually didn't last. The Berlin Wall for example. By their very nature, walls seemed to beg to be torn down by both sides of the place that it kept apart. The Great Wall of China on the other hand, didn't serve the defensive purpose that it once did but it was still standing proud and it was still stretching for miles and miles.

Purdue turned and nearly knocked a woman over who was suddenly standing right beside him. He hadn't noticed her before but she didn't seem bothered by the near collision. In fact, she was standing extremely close to him, only inches away. She was staring right at him and from the looks of it, she had been looking even before he almost smashed into her. She was flanked by two large men on either side of her.

She was an Asian woman with deep red lips, and those red lips tilted into an odd smile of recognition.

"David Purdue."

Purdue flinched at the sound of his own name. Someone knowing his name usually meant one of three very distinct options:

One, they were someone interested in the archaeological world and were a fan of his work but those kinds of people were few and far between. It wasn't like he had legions of fans chasing him all around public when he was seen. His work had a relatively small audience compared to many other lines of work.

Two, they were someone from his past travels that he had met but couldn't possibly remember. He had met hundreds if not thousands of people briefly over his many travels and it would have been impossible to store all of their faces in his memory.

The third and worst option was that it was someone with ill intentions; someone who was there specifically to find him and to do him harm. Given how the two men she was with were glaring at him, he had a feeling that it was option number three. Of course it was...he was rarely ever lucky enough for it to be option one or two.

"Can I help you?" He asked innocently despite his mind racing with different ways to defend himself from an ambush. He would see if conversation would lead to the truth before panicking. "Are you familiar with my work?"

"Not especially, no."

Well, that ruled out option number one and his hopes that he was about to make a fan's day.

"You are looking for the Great Khan's tomb."

She didn't ask it as a question. Instead, she stated it as a known fact. She knew exactly why he was there and that was another big red flag for him.

That certainly ruled out option number two as well. This wasn't a simple bystander from the past or a brief collaborator from a previous trip. This person was here because of his current goal, and that made it very obvious that he was face to face with option number three.

"Aye," Purdue said. "Maybe I am."

He glanced back to see where his teammates were and none of them were noticing the conversation he was having. Despite his suspicions, he really would have loved August to come barreling over. He could probably take both of the guys with this woman quite easily.

"But I doubt I'll find it," Purdue said with a shrug. "Many have tried. Many have failed. You also looking for it."

The woman's red lips twisted even more into an ugly sneer. "You have come to a very dangerous place, David Purdue."

"You keep saying my name. What's yours?"

"My name is Wai Lin. Your search is going to stop here, I am afraid. Right in the place where the wall should have been able to stop those Mongols' influence all those centuries ago."

"So who are you working for then?" Purdue asked, questioning both her and her two cronies. "Given that you even know about our search, I imagine Galen has been buying off some local assistance, is that it? That bastard is really starting to get annoying. How about you go back and tell that Irish shit that he's already caused me enough problems. I don't know what he's got going with August, or if there's even anything at all, but I'll beat him just like I always have."

Wai Lin frowned and surprisingly looked

confused by what most of what Purdue was saying. Before he had a chance to really wonder why, her scarlet smile returned to her face and she flashed a large grin.

"We will make you stop your search. Now."

Her two goons stepped forward and Purdue immediately retreated back a few steps before breaking into a full sprint away from them. He heard Wai Lin yell at them to follow him and Purdue called out to his team. Thankfully, despite the size of her men, they still had numbers on their sides.

"A little help, lads!"

August, Yusuke, and Riley all looked over from where they were examining the wall. He was impressed with how quickly all three of them came rushing to his aid. He was also very thankful for it, since before he could be brought down by his two opponents, he already got his reinforcements. August threw his large body at one of them, slamming against him and knocking the man straight off of the wall and falling down to the earth below. Yusuke held out an arm as he ran past and tripped the other onto his stomach. He then jumped onto the man's back and grappled him to the ground with Riley's help.

Purdue turned and couldn't help but smile. He looked toward where Wai Lin was standing and saw her trying to slink away. Luckily, Nina was right behind her, having been standing on the other side of her in her examinations of the wall. Purdue rushed to Nina with August but Nina already had it handled. Wai Lin tried to strike her but Nina caught her arm before she could hit her and held her steady.

"Really?" Nina asked through gritted teeth, trying to hold the woman's arm back. "Can't we have like five minutes of peace without people trying to kill us?"

Some tourists around them were watching with gaping mouths, looking nervous about whatever brawl had just broke out. Soon enough the authorities would come, so they had to get out of there with Wai Lin and her friend in tow. Purdue looked over the edge of the wall and saw Wai Lin's other lackey laying on the ground thirty feet below. He turned to August who shrugged his broad shoulders, looking guilty. "Didn't mean to push him quite that hard."

Purdue didn't smile. He knew that August was capable of killing people but he was so casual about it. That man had tried to hurt him, sure, but while the others had all managed to beat and capture their enemies without ending their lives, August had killed the man within seconds. He wasn't like the rest of them, that much was obvious

"Let's get out of here," Purdue said. "I have some questions I want to ask these two."

They led their prisoners down the wall and tried their best to ignore the muttering spectators who all looked terrified by what transpired.

Yusuke, thinking quickly on his feet, called out to the audience and started yelling out to them in their language. They all seemed to ease after his words and Purdue turned to him. "What did you say exactly?"

"That we are the police," Yusuke said. "That there is nothing to worry about and that these are bad people."

"Half a lie," Purdue said with a smile.

"Yes, and half a truth."

Some of the tourists on the wall actually started applauding as they led their prisoners by. Purdue was still impressed by how his team had reacted to threat, though August's method was a bit unnerving.

10

PICTURES FROM DAYS LONG PAST

They brought Wai Lin back to the suite along with her man. They got plenty of strange looks on their trek back to their room but Yusuke continued to calm people's nerves all along the journey. Once in the suite, they tied both of them to chairs but put them in two separate rooms. Yusuke took the man into the bathroom to question him, since the man seemed to not be able to speak English. Wai Lin had already proven to speak their language so Purdue felt confident in asking for answers from her. The only problem was getting her to actually give them anything useful.

"Who told you about us?"

Wai Lin tilted her head down but and just giggled under her breath. When she looked back up, that deep red smile returned.

"Why should I tell you anything?"

Nina   surprisingly   stepped   forward   and

smacked Wai Lin with the back of her hand. Everyone in the room looked taken aback, especially Wai Lin, whose red lipstick on her lips now streaked toward one of her cheeks.

"How dare you!"

Purdue turned to Nina and she gave an uncomfortable smile. "We need answers. Why hold back from getting them, yeah?"

Nina wasn't usually the type to get that violent with people. There were times when she had to of course but it usually wasn't without some real provocation or her defending herself from being killed. This seemed so sudden and without warning that she looked like she had surprised even herself. Maybe her long time spent as a prisoner of the Black Sun had changed her more than anyone thought. She was angrier now, even if she didn't always show it. Or maybe she wanted their attackers to be dealt with as quickly as possible just like Purdue did; she just might have been better about throwing around accusations but was just as upset about what happened to Shin Wo and about Galen's return.

"Galen Fitzgerald," Purdue said, leaning down toward where Wai Lin was sitting. "Know him? Short, ill-tempered bastard with an Irish accent. Sound familiar at all? Ringing any damn bells in your head?"

Wai Lin smiled again but her red smile was warped now from the smudge that Nina had made on her lips. It somehow made her look even more malicious, like her giddiness could stretch her grin even further than most human lips could go. She wasn't going to break easy, that much was obvious.

"I have never heard that name before in my life," Wai Lin said happily. "Never before. Not once. Not ever. Never, ever, ever."

Purdue's patience was thinning. He already assumed that it was Galen but he wanted to be sure. "Then who told you to come after us?"

"He did not tell me his name," Wai Lin laughed. "I do not know it. So you can hit me as much as you want, as much as it makes you happy, but it will not make any difference because I do not know the answers that you seek."

"You don't know his name?"

"No," Wai Lin snickered. "We do not ask for our clients names. They know that. It is part of why we have done such good business."

"Business?" August chimed in from behind them, stepping out of the shadows. He came up close, making Purdue a bit uneasy, but his towering shape loomed over Wai Lin threateningly. "Business and clients...so what are you some kind of hired gun then? Mercenaries?"

Wai Lin nodded. "I served the Triads for many years. I was good at finding people. I always found them. Anyone and everyone that I was supposed to. But that grew boring after many years so I decided to offer my services to others."

"And this man who hired you, wanted you to come for us?"

"He did," Wai Lin said, staring at Purdue. "He was very, very specific. He wanted it to be you, David Purdue. He had pictures and everything. A lot of pictures. So many angles and places and my, you are a good looking man from any one of those angles. From all directions."

Her taunts were grating on Purdue. She was the one being interrogated but she was enjoying it way too much. Somehow she had turned the tables and was the one holding all of the cards again. If they couldn't get a name out of her, then there wasn't much she could actually tell them. Then again, maybe they could figure out some answers from other things she had.

"You said he gave you pictures...do you still have them?" Purdue asked.

"I do, yes," Wai Lin snickered. "They are right over there." She nodded toward her little purse which Nina had tossed across the room when they came in. "It's all in there. We really must find out who took the pictures, they are works of art. Quite beautiful."

Purdue stepped away from their prisoner and walked over to her purse. He picked it up and rifled through it. It was a small bag so there wasn't much to rummage through before he found the thin stack of photos that were bunched together. He slid them out of the little purse and started to look them over carefully.

The picture on top of the stack was of him from a short distance away. It was a definitely a recent picture, taken during one of his visits to his rebuilt estate. So Galen was keeping an eye on his repaired mansion...that was creepy but made sense for an obsessed stalker like Galen. It was uncomfortable to know that he was being watched even in the comfort of his own home. Though, it was better than Julian Corvus crashing trucks through that house and invading it. At least Galen had the decency to stay a fair distance away and not make himself known.

He flipped to the next photograph and was startled by it. It was another snapshot of Purdue but he looked quite a bit different. He was in tattered clothes, had grown his beard out, and looked grimy and miserable. It was from after his money had been taken and his home had been burned to the ground. It was during the period of time where Julian and the Black Sun thought they had killed him. It seemed so long ago, but it was back when he had nothing to his name and was just a dead man begging for scraps on the streets.

The strange part was that as far as he knew, Galen hadn't known that he was alive back then. He seemed just as shocked as the rest of his enemies when he revealed that he was still alive. Had he known the whole time? Had he just pretended to be surprised when Purdue was revealed to still be kicking around? Maybe...it was possible that he did all that for show, but how had Galen known? And why didn't he immediately tell Julian back then?

It didn't make sense.

He kept looking through the pictures and was startled by just how much of a variety was from all kinds of different points in time. There were recent ones during his tenure as leader of the Black Sun. There were ones from a long time ago when, Nina, and Sam Cleave were all just starting to work together more frequently. There were even more from his time being 'dead' but he still couldn't fathom how Galen had seen him then. He had been being followed and spied on for years it seemed. The pictures were taken all over the world, from so many of his travels. Whoever was tailing him, had been incredibly good at staying hidden. He had no idea at any of those times that he was being monitored and tracked. It was baffling that Galen had been having him followed for so long. It still didn't quite add up.

His confusion and horror on his face must have been visible because Nina came up and looked over with him, gently scratching his back to sooth him. When she saw some of the pictures though, she gasped herself. "Oh my god."

"A bit odd, aye?" Purdue shook his head and showed her more of them. "Apparently I have a very big fan. Or I'm just a magnet for every camera on this planet."

Nina took one of the older pictures and

looked it over. "This was so long ago. Look at us. Galen was keeping tabs on us even then?"

"It seems so," Purdue said. "I always thought he was a bit clingy when we'd cross paths. And obviously I've come to realize just how jealous he was of me but this...I didn't expect him to be this creepy about the whole thing." Purdue turned back to the bound woman who had been enjoying his discomfort while looking at the pictures.

"So this client of yours...was he Irish?"

"I didn't ask."

"Did he have an accent!? And Irish accent!?" Purdue was at the end of his patience with her.

"I couldn't tell you," she said with a grin. "All I can tell you, is that he said you that you were looking for Genghis Khan's bones and that I was to find you and put you down. Oh and that I should make sure you were aware of what was happening. He wanted me to say your name and tell you that I knew what you were doing. Then the two I was with were going to throw you over the wall. Splat. That was the plan. Hate when things don't work out like you expect."

So his theory about the method was right. Part of their job was to get his attention first. That was certainly a Galen move. She might not know if the man who hired her was Irish but the more he was learning about this whole thing, the more it sounded like something Galen would absolutely do.

The only part he couldn't understand was that Galen took the time to speak to him in Mongolia just to tell him that they would meet again soon, to let him know that he was coming for him. Why send a few hired guns to go finish him off after putting in all of that effort? He could have at least given the task to Oniel. That was the only thing that didn't add up. The whole job sounded petty and cheap enough for Galen, but he couldn't imagine that he would have wanted three random hitmen to be the ones to end Purdue. He would have wanted that for himself.

"So what do we do with her?" Nina asked.

That was an interesting question that was going to have to be considered. Purdue wasn't very comfortable with an execution, but if they let her go, she would probably report to Galen about everything that happened. He didn't want Galen having that heads up and he would prefer that Galen not know exactly what had happened to the mercenaries that he sent after them.

Then again, it might not even matter. Based on those pictures, they were under extremely heavy surveillance at all times of the day no matter where they were. Galen probably already knew exactly what happened and probably even where they were.

Wai Lin looked up expectantly, like she was daring Purdue to give the order to end her life. She wasn't fooling him; he could see past her smeared red smile. He could see the hint of fear in her eyes. She was putting on a pretty good brave face but it wasn't enough to completely shroud her real feelings. She hadn't expected to lose. She thought that this would be easy probably. All she had to do was just kill a Scotsman on the Great Wall. It should have been a simple task—too simple. Why even confront him and not just kill him on the spot? Maybe that was part of the command...it would make sense for Galen. It was typical of him to need to make it known what was about to happen instead of just getting it done and over with. He always had to make his presence known.

"Want me to...?" August raised his brow and insinuated killing her. Purdue was once again somewhat disturbed by how quick and how open August was to suggesting doing the deed. It was off-putting to see just how comfortable he continued to be with taking a life, just like how he was with the man he so callously pushed off the top of the Great Wall.

"No," Purdue finally said. "We're not going to kill her."

Wai Lin couldn't hide her surprise and was even worse at hiding her relief.

"Y-y-you're not going to...?"

"Nope," Purdue said with a shrug. "It would be pointless. They already know all about us anyway. We wouldn't accomplish anything but wasting time and wasting a life. We're not the bad guys. The Order of the Black Sun no longer kills people so cavalierly. That's not how we operate. Even when it comes to terrible people like you lot."

The bathroom door opened and Yusuke walked out. He looked sullen but nodded to them. "The guy was some sort of assassin. He didn't know who was the one that gave him the contract but he did say it was a man. That was all he knew...oh and apparently they have been following you for a long time--"

"Thank you for all of the valuable information, Yusuke," Purdue said teasingly. "We got that exact same information from her minutes ago."

"Oh," Yusuke said and looked from them to Wai Lin. "And here I thought you were guys were going to be so pleased by my work."

"You just need to work on your timing, that's all, aye? That's it. Do that, and you're golden."

"Duly noted, fearless leader," Yusuke said and gave a mocking salute. "So...I don't have to kill him in there right? Truth be told, I've never...you know...taken someone out...put them to rest...any of that..." He scratched his hand uncomfortably but then turned to August. "You want to do it for me, big man?"

August grimaced embarrassingly, like he realized that everyone looked at him as the murderer of the group. In some ways, he kind of was. He was at least the one who was willing to mess people up the most. Still, he shook his head with a resounding no. "Purdue says that we're going to let them go."

"Really?" Yusuke looked a little confused but nodded. "Okay, okay. I'll go tell the guy tied up on the toilet the good news." Yusuke went back into the bathroom.

Purdue turned back to Wai Lin. "I just want to let you know that if you try coming for us again, this going to end a whole lot differently. I'm not going to forgive twice, understood? Am I clear?"

"Very clear," Wai Lin said. "We won't bother you again. It was a bad job to begin with." Purdue cut Wai Lin free and she got up. Surprisingly she gave Purdue a peck on the cheek, leaving behind some of her red lipstick. "I appreciate that you let me live. I will not forget it."

She moved to take the pictures back but Purdue held onto them and refused to let them go. "These are mine," Purdue said. "Consider them payment for not letting August beat you to death."

Wai Lin raised her hands in defeat. "Understood. You keep them. And if you see my client, let him know that we have no interest in working with him again. This was far more trouble than it was worth to us."

Wai Lin and her accomplice left the room, leaving Purdue and his team standing about. Purdue was going back through the pictures trying to figure out just how long Galen had been watching him. It was still unbelievable.

"I hope that was the right decision," August said. "We're giving them another chance to get back up and hit us harder and faster next time."

"It was," Purdue said. He felt a little anger just over August questioning him about it. August of all people shouldn't have been questioning anyone. He was lucky that he wasn't in handcuffs. He did as Nina advised and tried to keep calm, trying to stay focused on Genghis Khan's tomb. They had been distracted by Galen enough. They needed to get back to trying to find it. "Tell me again what the transcription of the markings on the bow said."

Riley stepped forward. She looked proud to be delivering it again, knowing that she was the one who found it to begin with. "The conqueror rests at the farthest reach, at the end of the red line."

Purdue went over it in his mind. He hadn't given that riddle quite as much thought as he would have liked. He had gone to the places that many others had gone looking for Genghis Khan. There were the places that everyone assumed he would be buried; by his home near the Odon River in Mongolia or some place of some importance like the Great Wall. Those places weren't the farthest reach, that was for sure. The farthest reach...Khan's reach...?

"The farthest reach," Purdue spoke aloud, trying to let the phrase germinate in his mind. "The farthest reach. The farthest reaches of his empire? Of the Mongol's reach...? How far did they get? The Mongol Empire?"

"They pushed through a large part of Europe after Genghis Khan's death," Nina said. "We're talking a fair distance inward on their advance and they might have even gone much further if they didn't withdrawal back to Mongolian when the current Khan died that year."

"Which year?" Purdue asked. "And where were they?"

"1241," Nina explained. She was fantastic at knowing dates like that for historical events. She could withdrawal them from her brain with ease and share them confidently. "And as for where, well...I believe they were somewhere near Hungry when they withdrew. They had already cut through Russia, Poland, and Germany when they had to go back home."

"All because their Khan died? They had to stop?" Riley asked.

Yusuke took over an explanation. "The leaders all had to be present for the choosing of another Khan. The deaths of Great Khan's had enormous impacts on the empire, as you could probably tell from Genghis Khan's own death."

"Exactly," Nina said. "And that was as far as their advance ever got before the succumbed to infighting and crumbled under their own weight. So if that's the farthest reach that they're talking about...then I suppose we should be going to somewhere around there...somewhere in the Hungarian Planes."

"That doesn't make sense," Purdue spoke up. "Not a lick of sense."

"Those are just the facts," Nina said with a shrug. "Sometimes fact don't make sense."

"That's not what I mean," Purdue said, waving her off as he took center stage in the middle of the group again. "I'm sure all of your facts were on point, Nina. What doesn't make sense is that the bow talks about Genghis Khan's remains being taken to the farthest reach. So yes, they could mean over in Europe but that doesn't add up to me."

"Why not?" Riley asked, looking befuddled by the whole conversation.

"Because that was over a decade after Khan's death. I imagine they buried his body much earlier than that. Soon after he passed probably."

"But that would be the farthest reach..." Nina said, obviously not yet seeing the point he was trying to make. "It says that the conqueror is buried at the farthest reach and to follow the red line. That part's obvious I think. The red line would be the trail of blood that the Mongols left in their wake."

"I agree with you there," Purdue said. "But the transcription never specifies that it's the Mongol Empire's reach that we're looking for. They got further after Genghis Khan's death, sure, but this bow seems to be talking specifically about

Genghis Khan in all regards to me. It's not talking about the reach of the Mongol Empire a decade and a half later. It's talking about Genghis Khan's reach."

"What are you saying?" August asked, scratching his head.

"I'm saying that I think we have the right idea here. I think we're right on about the farthest reach being the military reach of a conqueror like Khan. I think we're right about the red line being specifically about bloodshed. I think we're right on about the riddle...we're just looking at the wrong place. We should be thinking about how far Genghis Khan reached, not his children and grandsons and all the other descendants after him. That would make the most sense to me."

"So where would that be?"

Purdue remembered the stories that Shin Wo had told him, about the legend of Genghis Khan and his many deeds. There was one specific part that stuck in his mind; the last days of the Great Khan and how the circumstances of his death were uncertain. One of the things that was certain, was his last victory against the Western Xia Empire.

"Certainly not Europe," Purdue reiterated. "No, Genghis Khan never got that far. He died during his conquests of China. Most people agree that he died around the time of the fall of the Western Xia, if I remember right."

They all looked to one another uncertainly.

Purdue didn't sound entirely confident with his theory, he knew that, but he hoped they at least saw his point. It was a hard decision though; if they made the wrong choice, then it could take them on a long path leading to nothing but a waste of time. It would be a detour that would probably sap any of the energy they had left. The entire search could hinge on the decision of where they should be going next.

Nina seemed to be warming up to the idea. "It's a risk obviously," she said. "But you could be right, I guess. If that was where he fell, then they might have buried him nearby. He may have never gone back home."

Riley agreed, clapping her hands together. "It works with what we know from the bow I found. The last place that he was trying to take over before he did. That was Genghis Khan's reach. And the blood he was famous for spilling during his takeover...that would be the red line that the bow was talking about. It fits pretty perfectly."

It still would work quite well if it was talking about the Mongol Empire in general, Purdue thought, but kept that notion to himself. Nina was right that it was a risky decision to make, but it had to be made, one way or another. The Europe idea didn't make sense to him, but it was still a possibility.

"It just makes more sense for him to be buried some place that he actually got to," Purdue said, trying to put in his last arguments for his case. "His farthest reach. I don't think he would be buried as far as his empire got after his death. He would be buried near wherever he died. It just works."

When laid out like that, his whole team started to nod in agreement. He was glad they were hearing him. Things were tense, with all of the surprise attacks; whether they were from Shin Wo's killer or Wai Lin and her mercenaries that had tried to go after them. Even with the suspicion levied on August that made things so tense with everyone, they all could start to agree on something.

"Okay," Nina said, glancing to the others to see if they agreed. "We'll keep following your lead."

"Unless you lead us off of a cliff," Yusuke said with a smirk.

Purdue was thankful for their trust but still not sure that he was even right. He could be leading them the wrong way. They had checked the safe places so far for the bones; the mountains that every other previous searcher had tried to find the bones at. They had tried the Great Wall of China where he didn't expect to find anything anyway. And now, they were going someplace new, but with just as high of a chance that there would be nothing of value to find. He hoped he was right. He had only been leading the Order of the Black Sun for a short amount of time...he needed a win. He needed to prove that he was the right person to follow.

Purdue glanced down at the pictures that had been taken of him by some mysterious photographer. It was unfathomable that he had no idea during any of those times that he was being watched, but here was proof that he had been blind to someone on his tail. He had another shadow following him and he had had no idea that it was even there at all. He glanced out the window, nervous that another picture was being taken right now.

GALEN PUT DOWN THE PHONE. His contact had given him an update on David Purdue's next destination. Instead of digging up Mongolian canyons like everyone else had, Purdue was going to be exploring a part of China that not nearly as many people had searched. Even Galen knew that Genghis Khan's tomb was never found, but most people assumed that he was buried somewhere in Mongolia. It was interesting that he would have been buried some place that he conquered rather than back home, but it made sense in a way. A famed conqueror like him might want to be laid to rest in a place that he had just made his.

Oniel was nearby, waiting to hear the outcome of the phone call Galen just had. Galen turned to him, still a little annoyed by Oniel's impatience, but he managed a smile. He knew Oniel was itching to take a real shot at Purdue and his friends. Oniel had wanted to cut Purdue's throat since the day Purdue killed his brother. This was a long time coming, and he knew Oniel wanted it to be done and over with. He didn't care about the semantics or the details that Galen did. Galen's vengeance was going to be well-planned, drawn out, and relished. If Oniel got his way, then his vengeance would be swift, bloody, and messy. Galen wanted David Purdue slowly crushed and begging for mercy while Oniel just wanted Purdue stuck like a pig.

But if the information was correct, then there was apparently a high chance that Purdue was going to find the tomb of Genghis Khan soon. Once he did, Galen would be fine dispensing with him—after enjoying the moment, of course —and would appease Oniel's hunger for murder.

Galen hadn't thought too much about what would happen after he killed Davy, especially when it came to what would happen to the order. He imagined that he would have to kill or at least maim the new recruits that Purdue had brought into the Order of the Black Sun. They were probably chosen because they were loyal and a lot like Purdue. They wouldn't be of much use to Galen if they were angry with him for killing the man who brought them in. There were surely others who were still part of the order that didn't like Purdue and would want someone like Galen taking charge. They would love him for getting rid of Purdue. Then he could always call back some of the others that had fled the order like he did when Purdue took control.

If everything went well, Davy would be dead, the tomb of Genghis Khan would be found, and Galen would be able to become the undisputed leader of the Order of the Black Sun just like he wanted. Both David Purdue and Julian Corvus would be out of the way. It would make all of this, all of his struggles and embarrassments, worth it in the end if he ended up on top. They would all respect him and he would finally get the recognition that he deserved, with all of the people that pissed him off out of the way.

"Good news, my friend."

Oniel perked up, looking even more ravenous than usual.

"You know the time I was telling you to be so patient for?"

Oniel nodded.

"Well, it seems that time has come."

Oniel smiled.

INTERLUDE – THE STRONG MAN

August had heard all about "the fly" that kept getting in the way of all of the Order of the Black Sun's plans. Julian Corvus had gone on and on about the billionaire David Purdue and how he refused to die. He'd heard about Purdue so much, that he felt like he already knew the man well. The whole order seemed fixated on getting rid of him. It didn't help that Julian had an obsession with Purdue and so many of his plans and commands seemed to center on him.

So as August stood there, hearing that Julian had been beaten by Purdue, he didn't know quite how to feel. Many of his fellow members of the Order of the Black Sun were more than a little stressed. Many had immediately fled, hoping that they wouldn't go down with the sinking ship. August wasn't so quick to panic. He preferred to stay calm and see how things panned out before. Julian's defeat sent the order into chaos and he was curious to see how the group would look after the storm had passed. There might no longer be an Order of the Black Sun at all anymore.

Soon after they heard about Julian's defeat, rumors that David Purdue wanted to take control of the Black Sun started to reach them. Many of the members didn't believe those rumors, thinking Purdue would be crazy, suicidal even, to try and lead a group that had just tried to murder him. Some even said that if it was true, they wouldn't let Purdue lead for long.

When Purdue and his friends came to the compound, August watched them all closely. He recognized Nina Gould from her time as their prisoner and it was honestly strange to see her with so much freedom, not behind cell bars or in handcuffs.

Seeing Elijah Dane was something of a surprise too. Some people said that the Black Sun curator had defected, turned on Julian, and joined Purdue but many refused to believe that. Elijah was the one that they all gave the spoils of their searches to. Everyone knew him. He and the deep vaults he worked in were practically the hub of the order since every member went there repeatedly when they would come back to base after a long mission. It was baffling to most to even imagine Elijah being a turncoat. August wasn't surprised by it, though. He didn't know Elijah very well but he could always tell that the curator wasn't actually happy with having to serve Julian. He was passionate about his work with the artifacts—that much was obvious—but it was also apparent that Elijah wasn't helping the Black Sun by choice. So seeing him come back to the compound at Purdue's side and as one of his pals wasn't a shock for August.

However, he was a little surprised by David Purdue when he finally saw him in person. Given how much trouble he caused the order, August expected Purdue to be some seven foot tall, muscular giant with a chiseled face like some action hero from the movies. Instead, there wasn't anything overly special about Purdue's appearance. He wasn't nearly as formidable looking as August imagined and he was sure that he could easily tear him apart in a fight. He didn't understand what all of the fuss was about but there must have been more to him since he was capable of not only evading the Order of the Black Sun, but defeating them. And now the one man that should have been easy to bring down was going to dismantle and reorganize the organization that he fought for so long. He couldn't have been as normal as he seemed.

Throughout the next week, as the new leadership settled into their new roles, many of the other members left the order in protest. They complained, and stewed, and threw threats around. August didn't leave, and he didn't waste his breath whining like so many of the others did.

There was no point. This was the way the Order of the Black Sun was now sometimes you just had to roll with the punches, even if it was still doing some damage to take the hits.

Naturally, Purdue wasn't giving many good assignments to established members. He probably didn't trust them, and maybe he was right. Whatever the case, August sometimes felt like a relic of a bygone era, even though that era had ended only weeks earlier. It was a sudden change of pace for the order but he did his best to adapt to his new environment.

The only thing he missed was some of the action he used to get to be a part of when Julian was in charge. It wasn't that he liked hurting people or inflicting pain. He wasn't some sort of sadist or anything like that. He liked how alive a fight made him feel. It was simple and he liked things being simple. August wasn't entirely sure how to feel about Purdue as a leader yet. He had never been afraid of Julian like so many other people were but he had to admit it was nice having a boss that wouldn't kill you on a whim.

He understood the tension between the few remaining agents and their leader but he didn't really share their animosity. Still, it made sense that Purdue kept anyone who used to work for Julian at arms' length. He needed to avoid a civil war between the members that would cause the entire operation to implode in on itself.

August accepted that he was part of the vets,

pushed out of the way in favor of the bright new recruits. They were far less violent and were a symbol of a brighter future. Of course Purdue would favor them and give them the more fruitful ventures.

That made it more surprising when August was brought onto the team that was going to find Genghis Khan's tomb. He never expected to get that assignment and couldn't even begin to figure out why that had even happened. He certainly wasn't qualified academically. He knew next to nothing about Genghis Khan other than the name and that he was some great warrior. The only reason he could think of was that he was brought along for the muscle. He was going to be the strong guy of the group. He wasn't going to be brought on for anything other than that, and he was okay with that. At least Purdue was finally willing to work with him.

And August would do his best to prove that he still have something to contribute to the Order of the Black Sun.

11

RAINFALL ON STONE

Their plane landed in Yinchaun, a city that was once the capital of the Western Xia empire of the Tanguts. They were the last enemies that Genghis Khan faced before his death. His demise had even supposedly happened during the fall of the city after his victory. That must have been unfortunate, to have won the battle but lost the war with mortality in in the very same day. It was a bittersweet end for the successful conqueror, but fitting that he had died during a conquest.

The city was a modern metropolis now, with about two million people living there, and was built right beside the Yellow River. It wasn't one of the more famous cities of the world, not even of China and seemed like a strange choice to put Genghis Khan's remains but if the riddle was right, then he was resting at the farthest reach of his army. This was as far as they got with Genghis

Khan as their leader. The Mongol Empire had moved on to Europe but Purdue had a gut feeling that they wouldn't have brought the first Great Khan's body that far. They would have put him in the place where he fell, and that was right here near Yinchaun.

The others weren't entirely convinced by his argument but he imagined most of them just wanted an excuse to go back to Europe, closer to home where things made the most sense. The only real support he had for this change in direction was Yusuke, who agreed with him that the Mongolians never would have put Genghis Khan's resting place in Europe. Even here, in Yinchaun, they were still relatively close to Mongolia. It was on the other side of the Helan Mountain range that nestled parts of the city.

If they were following the proverbial red line as directed, and following the trail of the blood to his grave site, then this was the natural endpoint. The fall of Yinchaun was the last slaughter that Genghis Khan took part in. This was where his bloodletting was put to a sudden halt.

They decided to book a hotel for the night so they could all be well rested. As nice as the city was, Purdue didn't think that the tomb was within it. He had determined that the most likely place for the tomb was outside of the city in the Helan Mountains. It was a secluded area that would be hard to traverse and even harder to find, a safe place to protect his burial site. But if they were going to take on those mountains, they would need to be at full strength. That meant a good meal and a good sleep.

"Think Galen is following us?" Nina asked as they got off the plane.

"Most likely," Purdue said. "You saw the pictures. He's apparently been trailing us all over creation without us having a clue. How could we not have seen that, aye? He's a lot smarter than I ever gave him credit for, I suppose."

"Well we'll be ready for him this time," Nina said. "And it's not going to be like with that mercenary from the Great Wall this time, right? We need to put him down for good. You've let him go before. You've let Oniel go. They keep coming back and don't learn from it. You know me, Purdue. You know I'm not usually so quick to be begging for someone's death but they honestly deserve it. They don't deserve any more chances because all they have ever done is completely waste them."

"I know, Nina," Purdue said and had already came to that determination himself.

When the time came, Galen and Oniel would both have to be killed. It was the only way to stop their threat for good. If they were allowed to keep on living out there in the world, they had shown that their hatred for Purdue and his friends would only continue to fester until there was nothing they could do about them. They were a threat, and if they got any angrier, they might be a threat to a whole lot more people than they already were.

That night, everyone enjoyed the finest meal that the hotel could prepare for them. They all sat around the table and laughed. There was some underlying tension, but they managed to sweep it underneath the table for one night. Purdue didn't try to accuse August of treachery. Nina didn't bring up the great big elephant in the room known as Galen Fitzgerald. Yusuke and Riley remained just as pleasant as ever, keeping things light and fun.

For all they knew, the next day could be full of a whole lot of danger. Purdue had seen before how quickly an expedition could go from a nice, scenic trip to a life or death situation, and sometimes, not everyone made it back. They just had to enjoy the night and enjoy this time they had together, no matter what their differences were. Purdue actually relished that dinner, as it solidified his relationship with his new teammates on a social level. They didn't have to discuss the tomb of Genghis Khan. They didn't have to talk about Galen's threats. They could talk about all of the nice things that had gone in their lives.

Even August seemed slightly less suspicious while laughing around the table with them all. For the briefest moment, Purdue wondered if he might have been wrong, but he tucked that thought away. He couldn't afford to lower his guard when they were potentially getting so close to the end goal.

They all woke up late the next morning feeling full of food and rejuvenated from the cozy beds they slept in. It was a big step up from the arrangements they had for the rest of the expedition. A dark part of Purdue's humor appreciated that Shin Wo was killed in the tent rather than later on when his blood would have made a big mess out of one of those hotel rooms. That thought made Purdue a bit sad, though, as if not for Galen, that old man would have probably been with them right now, probably excited that they were so close to finding Genghis Khan.

The whole team dressed and packed for a rough hike. The Helan Mountain range didn't look like it was going to be a nice stroll up a hill. It was going to be a tough, challenging hike and they would have to climb all over to figure out if the tomb was somewhere within its cliffs. It wouldn't be easy and it might even have taken days so they were sure to bring along sleeping bags for that eventuality.

They hopped onto a shuttle that took them out toward the mountains and away from the city. As Purdue looked back at that pleasant little city, he realized how much he was going to miss that night at the hotel. Things had seemed so nice for that brief period of time. Now they were trekking out into the wild again, where all kinds of circumstances might change for better or worse.

He looked to the tall mountains looming ahead, painted against the sky. He hoped with every fiber of his being that the tomb was there along with Genghis Khan's remains. He needed that conqueror found, it was the only way to prove to the rest of the order that they could all work together, and unite everyone just as Genghis Khan united all of those bickering Mongolian tribes.

Purdue wasn't sure yet how good of a leader he was but he knew he could be better, and the remnants of one of the world's most successful leaders might have been the perfect way to prove his own worth.

It was a good distance out away from civilization but once they hopped off of the shuttle, they immediately got to work on their hike. Purdue led the way but everyone was tasked with keeping their eyes out as best as they could for anything that looked out of the ordinary; for anything that might stand out and give them some kind of inclination if Khan really was resting somewhere there. Purdue really wished some beam of light would shine down from the heavens and point out where they needed to go within the mountain range but there was no such luck.

The Helan Mountains weren't the highest mountains on the planet but they were plenty high for a such a wide search. They hiked as best as they could up and down the cliffs, looking everywhere they could for the tomb. There was so much ground to cover and nightfall came very quickly.

That night wasn't a comfortable one, unlike their hotel sleep. The rocky terrain and cold temperatures weren't the best conditions to fall asleep in. The night dragged on and on for Purdue, whose body just refused to let him get any rest. He lay there all night, staring up at the stars wondering how he could feel so far from the tomb when his head told them that they were getting close.

Then there was that teeny, tiny part of his mind that suggested that the tomb of Genghis Khan might not even be real at all and that it had been nothing more than a legend that had been passed down for generations. People loved romanticizing leaders of old, and making them seem more mythical than historical. All of the stories about his death and his burial might not even be true after all. He hoped that wasn't the case but it was indeed possible. But he refused to accept that as a viable scenario. He had experienced doubt on things that were much more outlandish than this journey and those had even turned out to be real.

Purdue didn't sleep that night, torn between feelings of doubt and hope. When they all woke up the next morning, they set through more of the mountains. They looked in caves. They looked under trees and stumps. They looked on the peaks of some of the summits and they looked in the valleys that had formed between them. There was a still a lot more of the Helan Mountains to see but they were all starting to lose a bit of hope.

Some of them like Purdue even felt somewhat guilty. If it turned out that Genghis Khan really had been buried out in Europe where his empire had reached long after his death, then Purdue had wasted all of their times by coming here. He might have taken them down the completely wrong path and completely ignored his adviser's thoughts when it came to the site of the burial.

There were also little pockets of civilization within the mountain range that they could see in the distance sometimes. Nina was quick to explain that in recent years this particular mountain range had become the hub for some wine development in China. It was only after authorities had allowed it but companies were now making it a good place for wine production. So at the very least, if they couldn't find an eight hundred year old dead world conqueror up in these mountains, they could still at least possibly find something good to drink away their sorrows of defeat.

The sun was starting to set already after another long day of searching but not before they could all see a big plateau up ahead. A wall of rocks circled around a raised portion of land on all sides. There would be no way to walk up to the top of that. They would have to scale the face of that rock and climb.

"That's a distinctive looking place," Riley said. "I kind of love it. It's beautiful."

"Do you think the people that buried him thought he same thing?" Nina asked. "Maybe that would be the perfect place to put him."

The group of them marched toward the plateau ahead as the sun drifted away behind the mountains and dark clouds took its place. Light rain started falling down on them as they got closer, almost like the universe was telling them not to even try getting up there. They reached the enormous wall of rock that made up the side of the plateau and all looked up uneasily. It would be a long climb to reach the summit, especially when the rocks were going to be slippery from the water pouring out of the clouds.

"We should wait until morning," Nina said over the sound of rain. "We should wait for the weather to clear up and for some sunlight."

"Who knows when the rain will stop?" Purdue countered. If Genghis Khan really was up there, then he wanted to get up there as soon as possible. "It could be awhile..."

"Then let's at least wait for some light. We want to be able to see where we're putting our hands while we're climbing, don't we?" Nina asked.

He could tell that she had the support of the others behind her. As much as Purdue wanted to keep arguing his point and as much as he wanted to hurry up and get to the top, he knew that Nina was right. Rain was already a dangerous factor to add to the climb but mixing in rain, and not being able to see where you should be putting your limbs was a not only a very bad combination, but also could be potentially become a possibly lethal one.

"Aye," Purdue said. "We'll wait until first light then we'll get all of our asses up that plateau. And we'll all make it in one piece."

Everyone seemed relieved by his decision and he was surprised that they thought he would ever force them to climb up a height like that in bad weather. Maybe they really didn't think that much of him as a leader after all but he wasn't going to let that bother him. He knew he was at least better as leader of the Black Sun than Julian had been. Julian would have killed every single member of the team by now, probably just for fun or for even the slightest bit of disagreement.

They managed to find a tree to put their bags under and did their best to ignore the rainfall pelting them as they slept. It was an even rougher night of sleep than the night before. Purdue couldn't wait for them to get back to civilization, or at least to nice beds. That night at the hotel in Yinchuan had completely spoiled him.

They got up the next morning to find that it was still raining, just a little bit less hard than it was the night before. Nina and the others still seemed nervous but Purdue was determined that this would be the day. They would just have to be more careful than they usually would have. Luckily, Purdue came prepared for a possible tough climb and brought cables to connect everyone. In case someone fell, the others' combined strength should be enough to keep them from plummeting to an early grave.

The climb was a difficult one, and Purdue usually thought of himself as a fairly good climber. The plateau's sides weren't meant to be climbed and finding good places to put your hands and get a grip was harder than Purdue ever expected. The rain certainly didn't help as it made things even slicker and harder to grasp.

The others were actually starting to get ahead of him and Purdue watched them all climbing above him, feeling somewhat embarrassed. There was nothing to actually feel bashful about but just the principle that he was supposed to be leading this climb and was the one most anxious for the climb but he was the one falling behind.

Purdue made a mistake and glanced down over how high they were and petrified by just how far they had gotten. If one of them did fall, it was going to be a long way down and their body would be nothing but a flat strip of flesh after it found the bottom. He really wished he hadn't done that because now his body was shaking even more. He needed to stay steady and stable, and keep a firm grip on everything he touched.

Their long climb wasn't done as the sun set yet again over the Helan Mountains. The rain started to fall harder again and Purdue was getting pelted by water running down the cliff side. Drops that were slipping off his friends ahead of him smacked him straight in the face. He squinted and tried to push himself to keep going for as long as he possibly could but he was really struggling.

"I can see the top!" Yusuke's voice just barely managed to carry over the sound of rainfall. In the darkness of the night, it was hard for Purdue to see the top but he was glad that someone could. It meant this terrible climb was almost at an end and he could stay on two solid feet again. "I can see it!"

There were whoops and hollers from the others but Purdue didn't have the energy to join in to the celebration. He just wanted off this terrible mountain, and the quicker they found Genghis Khan, the quicker they could leave. He just dreaded the notion that they had scaled this plateau for no good reason. He really, really hoped that Khan was up there waiting for him.

Purdue watched Yusuke disappear over the cliff side at the top and the others were getting close too. Even he was well on his way to being able to stop climbing. It was just going to be a little bit longer and then he would be standing upright again. He was only a few more strides away from the top. He couldn't wait.

The others had all reached the top and disappeared over the edge. Soon enough, he would be up there with them.

In his sudden burst of excitement, Purdue missed the rock he was trying to grab and felt his whole body slip for a second. He lunged out to quickly replace his grip and fond very, very sharp stones. Purdue held on for dear life but the rocks were incredibly sharp and he had to keep a good grasp on them to not fall. They dug into his finger sand he could feel warm blood flowing down the side of his hand.

August was crouched above him, at the edge of the cliff. The big man looked down at him and Purdue couldn't tell what he was thinking. The others had already made it to the top. They probably couldn't hear him or had any idea that there was any sort of trouble at all. It was just him and August—the person that he trust the least of all in the group—and the person that he had accused of treachery and murder. If he was wrong, then August was probably pretty upset with him. If he was right, well then this was the perfect chance for August to finish the job.

August's expression was impossible to read and his intentions were more than a little unclear because of it. If he wanted Purdue gone, this was a perfect opportunity. Purdue was helpless and clinging for life in the middle of a storm. With how wet the rocks were, he honestly felt like he could easily slip and fall to his death. August probably wouldn't even have to push him in conditions like that. This was his chance. If he was still loyal to the old Black Sun, he could kill Purdue and play it off as an accident.

August's great big hand came toward his wrist and Purdue could see his own death flashing before his eyes. August would pry his bloody hands off of those rocks and Purdue would tumble down into the abyss. He felt those dark hands do exactly as he envisioned and wrap around his wrist. Purdue winced as the grip tightened but instead of falling, he was heaved upward by August. The enormous man pulled him up the cliff until they were both standing. Purdue stared at August, baffled and August didn't say a word. He just gave a curt nod before walking away to rejoin the group.

Purdue thought he was going to die and he thought August would be his killer. It had been so possible in those moments but now it seemed ridiculous. He still didn't trust August by any means, but why would he kill him like that? If he had wanted to kill him like that, he would have done it by now.

"Thank you, August."

August looked at him hard. "You're welcome."

12

THE RESTLESS VOICES

The storm started to clear, and only left a few stray droplets of water. It was such odd timing that it felt like the storm was intentionally trying to make their climb even more stressful than it already was. The group walked across the plateau. It was just as Purdue imagined it would be at the top; a perfectly flat terrain that overlooked the surrounding lands. He could see Yinchaun in the distance, past a few other mountain peaks. And in the other direction, he could see Mongolia, Genghis Khan's homeland. If he was here, at least he was relatively close to home, but Purdue did not envy the people who buried him if they had to make that climb with a body in tow.

The plateau was a safe place to rest, that was for sure. Most people would never want to climb all the way up there. Purdue wished that he had charted a helicopter or a private plane to reach the plateau...it would have saved them a lot of trouble and saved him a few scares. But these mountains were a bit treacherous and might have been dangerous for aircraft to navigate. He expected at least someone from the team to have pointed out that other option but no one did, not even during the climb. They really were a determined group.

Riley suddenly came to an abrupt halt and Purdue nearly crashed into her. He was about to say something snarky but held back when he saw her expression. Her mouth was wide open and her eyes wide but she didn't seem to be looking at anything in particular. She was focused instead on one of her other senses.

"Did you hear that?"

"Hear what?"

Purdue looked around and cupped his hands around his ears, trying to hear whatever had startled her. He was hoping it was some kind of animal and not Galen on their trail again. He took a long minute just listening and his teammates did the same but they all looked just as confused as he was.

Riley looked rattled. Usually she seemed so carefree and full of energy, but all of that had just been sucked away in moments. The others had stopped trying so hard to hear and were just waiting to see who spoke first but Riley was still frozen, focused on her eardrums.

"What--"

"Shh." The sound barely left her but immediately made Purdue fall quiet. She was dead serious, far more serious than he had ever seen her act. She had really heard something—something bad.

Nina took a step closer to Purdue but was staring at Riley with concern. They all were looking at Riley with a lot of worry. Even August kept looking over his shoulder like whatever unhearable sound would reveal itself to startle him.

Still, there was nothing to be heard except for a light breeze passing by them at this height. That cold wind just made things even more tense. He couldn't hear whatever Riley was hearing, but things didn't feel quite right upon the plateau. There was nothing around them but earth, a long drop, and mountains surrounding area. There was nothing...so why did he feel like they weren't alone? He got the distinct impression that there was another group of people besides their group, gathering nearby. Maybe Galen and his team were close and he was going to follow through on those threats he had made back in Mongolia. Or maybe there was someone else, but something didn't feel right at all. He had only felt this strange sense of turmoil a few times before; usually in dark haunted places that he would very much never like to go to again.

Then he heard it too. It was somehow quiet but so loud at the same time. A shriek rang between his ears. It startled him so much that he nearly fell over. Then he heard another yell, and then another; multiple different voices crying out in terror and pain. It was like an entire crowd of people were all crammed inside of his head, screaming for their lives and begging for mercy.

He looked around, practically spinning in place trying to see any sign of where those horrible sounds could have even been coming from but there was nothing at all. They were alone up there on that plateau. There was no one screaming, not really. He knew it was only echoing in his mind—it still was—and it didn't seem to want to stop. He didn't even know if it would could. Maybe he'd hear those shrieks for the rest of his life and have no way to knock the sounds out of his ears and exorcise them from his brain.

His entire body shivered and he knew it wasn't just from the altitude. It was a visceral response to what he was hearing. He wasn't sure how real the screams were but they must have been at least somewhat actually there. He wasn't the only one who heard them. It wasn't just some trick of his imagination or some terrible dormant memory. Riley heard it too, and she was just as scared of it as he was starting to be.

"What is it?" Nina asked, her eyes brimming with concern. She put a comforting hand on Purdue's shoulder and asked again. "What's going on?"

He could barely hear her at all. Her voice was

almost completely drowned out by the endless screaming. The voices weren't speaking English. It was a language he didn't understand but the fear those shouts were filled with was more than good enough translation to know that something terrible was happening. Those voices were from people in real pain, probably even dying, and they were begging and pleading to survive, clinging desperately to life.

"What is it!?" Nina was practically shouting now. She shook Purdue's shoulders, trying to stir him back long enough to get an answer but Purdue couldn't. No matter how loud she got, she was still quiet in comparison to how loud these invisible people in his mind were. "What the hell is going on, Purdue!"

Purdue shut his eyes. The world around him felt like it was barely there anyway. He wished that closing his eyes stopped the screams but they continued, even more powerful once he was solely focused on his sense of hearing. There was no getting away from it, but Purdue began to feel that escaping these voices wouldn't do much good. He needed to understand them—to know exactly why this was even happening.

There was something else besides the yelling, something behind it. There was the sound of flesh being torn apart, of metal sinking into bodies. Those screams weren't just from fear, they were from the pain of peoples' last moments. These were the death cries of people being murdered—no—butchered. Something horrible had happened here, maybe somehow in some unseen plane, it still was. Victims lingering, tormented for centuries by the violence of their ends.

"Something happened here..." Purdue managed, wincing from the loud noises knocking around in his head. He spoke loudly, just to be sure that Nina and the others could even hear him. He looked around the plateau and started walking past his team. "Something awful."

He didn't know if his teammates were even following him, but he couldn't focus on that. He instead tried his best to follow the voices, and they seemed to grow louder once he started walking. He was being led somewhere by a trail of invisible blood, from a bloodletting that had taken place hundreds of years before.

It wasn't his mind playing tricks on him and it wasn't Riley's mind playing tricks on her. She walked up beside him and the two followed the sounds as best as they could. They both moved wearily, nearly falling over from the pain that was ringing in their heads.

Whispers came underneath the screams; collective chants that were growing louder and louder with each step he took. A dozen voices all saying the same word and he could hear that so vividly now. That one word confirmed their location and made it more than clear that they had reached their intended destination. The word that broke through the death thralls was "Khan."

Khan. Khan. Khan. Khan. Khan. Khan. Khan. Khan. Khan. Khan. Khan. Khan. Khan.

Purdue picked up his pace and he could feel Riley beside him. They somehow knew that if they could get to where these voices rang loudest, they might actually be able to get rid of them. They might somehow be able to free themselves from the sounds plaguing them.

Khan. Khan. Khan. Khan. Khan. Khan. Khan. Khan. Khan. Khan. Khan. Khan. Khan. Khan.

One step. Then another. They just have to keep moving.

Khan. Khan. Khan. Khan. Khan. Khan. Khan. Khan. Khan. Khan. Khan. Khan. Khan. Khan.

Purdue was off balance and reeling from everything going on inside of him. This was madness, possibly even real madness overcoming him.

Khan. Khan. Khan. Khan. Khan. Khan. Khan. Khan. Khan. Khan. Khan. Khan. Khan.

Just a little further but the steps were getting hard. Everything felt like it was disappearing except for the deafening screams and the name that continued to ring over and over. It was all that mattered now, the rest of the world seemed to disappear. He didn't know if his friends were still behind him. He barely knew if he was even actually going anywhere at all.

Khan. Khan. Khan. Khan. Khan. Khan. Khan. Khan. Khan. Khan. Khan. Khan. Khan. Khan.

Purdue would feel completely alone if he couldn't feel Riley moving beside him. He was glad she was there too, and he was glad that both and her weren't insane after all. Then again, maybe they were. Maybe this was some sort of shared mental breakdown into lunacy. But if that was the case, at least they had each other. At least they wouldn't drown in madness alone.

Khan. Khan. Khan. Khan. Khan. Khan. Khan. Khan. Khan. Khan. Khan. Khan. Khan. Khan.

There was something large up ahead, looming over them in the middle of the plateau.

Khan. Khan. Khan. Khan. Khan. Khan. Khan. Khan. Khan. Khan. Khan. Khan. K--

The screams and chanting in his mind ended abruptly, like they had just been immediately silenced once Purdue saw that shape ahead.

Then one last shout, but it was more like a roar of angry voices. It was louder than any other of the others had been and far more clear. It seemed to shake the entire world around him when it came through his brain.

KHAN.

The name and the wave of voices hit Purdue like a wave and he felt himself falling forward, tipping over straight down toward the rocks at his feet. In seconds, his head collided down onto the hard terrain and all of the wind was sucked out of his body.

Everything went black for a moment, but only for a moment.

Purdue opened his eyes and found himself still laying in the middle of the plateau, high above so much of the surrounding area. He looked around and saw that the object he saw ahead was some sort of giant rock, but didn't find anyone that he recognized. Riley was no longer beside him. Nina, Yusuke, and August had completely vanished. But despite the disappearance of his allies, Purdue saw that he wasn't alone on this rock after all.

A line of frail, skinny men were turning away from a group of other men. The other group were well dressed, looked much better fed, and were all armed. Their weapons were drawn on the skinny men who all turned and started to flee. All of their faces were petrified with panic and fear. They ran toward Purdue and he held out his hands and called out but they ignored him. Some ran right past him while others were cut down by the armed group of men.

He didn't know how but something was pushing ideas into his head. He had no way of confirming what he was thinking but he somehow knew exactly what he was seeing. Those skinny men running for their lives were slaves whose lives had been forfeited to the Mongol conquerors that took their homes. The ones doing the killing were soldiers of Genghis Khan, trying to kill any witnesses to the Great

Khan's burial site. They had ambushed these slaves without any sort of warning or reason and were going to kill every last one of them, to bury the secret with Khan.

Purdue watched as the slaves were cut down without any sort of explanation. They all screamed, begged, and pleaded for mercy and he recognized all of those terrified shrieks that left their mouths; those same yells were the ones that had been filling every corner of his mind. They never stood any sort of chance against their masters. One of them, the last survivor tried to put up a fight but couldn't do much against a blade. He fell too and after all of the slaves were dead or dying, the soldiers all turned their weapons on themselves and committed suicide around that giant rock nearby. They were going to every possible length to get rid of anyone that knew where Genghis Khan was buried—and he had been buried just there—so close to where they had all fallen.

Purdue knew that was true. Some otherworldly presence was pushing him towards his answers, showing him and telling him what he needed to know. His gut told him it might have even been those slaves, their souls lingering on this plateau, haunting the place of their sudden deaths. Maybe they wanted to spite those guards that had tried too hard to protect Genghis Khan's burial place. It sure seemed like they were leading Purdue closer.

Purdue turned around and one of those personal guards were standing directly behind him. That warrior let out a roar and lunged forward with his blade. Purdue gasped and just as the blade pierced his chest, the vision he was in the midst of dissipated and he was blanketed by darkness again.

"Purdue!"

Pain seared through Purdue's face and he found himself laying on the rocks, surrounded by his team. There were no spectral slaves showing him their demises and there weren't any murderers warriors cutting down anyone. All of his allies were looking down at him, alive and well, looking none the wiser to anything that he had seen.

"Are you okay?" Yusuke asked.

He didn't know how to answer that. He wanted to believe that everything he had seen was just some concoction of his imagination when he had hit his head after the fall but he knew that wasn't the case. It had been far too vivid, far too detailed, and far too real. There was no way he could have ever just come up with that. He didn't have that good enough of an imagination. Most of all, he knew it based on the fact that Riley was lying next to him, looking rattled.

They met eyes and she nodded to him.

"I saw it too. I saw it all."

"Saw what?" Nina asked, probably more

forcefully than she intended but Purdue understood why. It was coming from a place of genuine concern. To the others, it had probably looked like he and Riley had shared some sort of psychotic episode. They couldn't understand the gravity of what they had both been through. They didn't know the full story like they did. And they hadn't gotten the confirmation that Purdue now understood—they had found it.

The tomb of Genghis Khan was so close—and his burial had been just as bloody as the rest of the conqueror's life. That much was clear enough. The rest of the world, the textbooks of history had no idea about this part of the story. No one else knew about the brutality that had taken place. Of the billions of funerals and wakes there had been in the history of mankind, very few had probably been as violent as this one. It was fitting; so fitting that it made Purdue a bit sad that the rest of the world didn't have a clue about the somewhat poetic nature of the very end of Genghis Khan's story. Maybe they would now, now that Purdue was going to find his remains.

"Someone mind telling me what's going on?" August asked, rubbing his hands together uneasily. "No one's saying anything! You're all freaking me the hell out."

"This is the right place," Purdue said. "Trust me." He turned to Riley. "Trust us."

The voices had stopped shouting and Riley even seemed to be returning to her usual self.

She was even smiling now, and not looking petrified. Purdue himself was starting to feel a little bit better. Whatever invisible force had dragged them toward this spot had done the work it wanted to apparently. They all took a minute to catch their breaths. It had undeniably been a long and hard journey but Purdue was feeling very hopeful now. He just hoped that these ghosts from the past were done using him as a compass. It hadn't been a very enjoyable experience. Hopefully, it was going to just be an easy end to this expedition now—but things hardly ever worked out the way he wanted. Maybe this would be the first.

13

THE REMAINS AND THE LEFTOVERS

The tomb was built under an enormous boulder that must have been there since long before Genghis Khan's burial. It seemed to work as something of a headstone for the grave—an enormous, solid marker fit for a man as powerful as Genghis Khan was. It wasn't ornate but it permeated strength and stability. They just had to make sure that he was actually buried there or this whole search had been for nothing. All of the clues they followed led to this spot. If it wasn't here, they would have to start all over and go straight back to the drawing board.

Purdue and the others got to work and before long, they all have shovels in their hands and were digging all around the large rock. The excitement over this being the right place fueled them all with newfound vigor. There was a good chance that this was where they wanted to be and had finally reached their destination. They all felt so close to what they had worked so hard for. Something hidden from the world for eight centuries could be buried right beneath them.

Purdue had experienced this kind of sensation before in his travels but for some reason, this one seemed a little different, more potent than a lot of the others. Maybe it was because this would be his first big victory as the leader of the Order of the Black Sun. This would prove that his decision to restructure the secret society would be worth it; that a once malicious organization could actually be used for something positive for a change. This would show everyone that the Order of the Black Sun was not going to be different, but already was.

"Does this count as grave robbing?" Riley asked beside him, wiping some sweat from her brow and looking disgusted. "I feel like I need to take like fifty showers now."

"It's only grave robbing if there's actually a grave here."

"Great," she said, looking disgusted. "Now part of me hopes we don't find the tomb now."

HOURS WENT by and they all kept digging. There had to be something, anything to show that this was the right place. Those terrifying visions had to have meant something; it couldn't have been for nothing at all. He had seen those sights with his own eyes, he'd seen that massacre and heard the whispers of what that meant whispered into his ears. Purdue kept on shoveling, no matter how tired he got. With each chunk of dirt and earth he tossed aside, he could feel how close he was to Genghis Khan.

There was something there in the dirt, right by his feet. Purdue reached in and pulled it from the earth. It was a bone—possibly belonging to Genghis Khan. It wasn't for certain, but at the very least, he knew that this was indeed a burial site after all.

"Oi! Over here!"

He called out and everyone else stopped their shoveling for a minute to see what he found. They all looked over the bone with wide, optimistic eyes, and were all just as hopeful as he was that this was what they had come all this way for.

They kept digging in that general part of the ground and kept finding more and more remains, like pieces of a puzzle that they were trying to put together. With each part that they found, Yusuke starting laying the bones in place a few yards away, doing his best to construct a person on the ground. There were two hundred and six bones in the human body. Purdue didn't expect to find every single on of them. Some had probably crumbled to dust over the centuries since they had any sort of meat on them. They kept pulling the bone from the grave for hours.

Purdue took hold of a piece he saw and heaved. What came up was battered and withered but was very clearly a human skull.

It was him.

He was looking into the eye holes of one of history's most notorious and successful conquerors. Of course, no eyes were looking back at him. There were just two dark openings. He was thankful for that. Being in Genghis Khan's sights probably hadn't been a good thing.

He cupped the cranium in his grasp. One of the most recognizable names in the long history of mankind and here Purdue was, holding his head. It was surreal, to say the least.

"Is that...?" Yusuke was at his side, looking with amazement at the skull. He had been looking for Genghis Khan's remains far longer than Purdue had. "Is that really him?"

"Seems so," Purdue said. "But we won't know for sure until we can have these bones examined. But...who else would it be, aye?"

Yusuke looked beyond happy and Purdue shared that joy and relief. This wasn't all just for nothing. They had really found him. Shin Wo had been senselessly murdered in his sleep but his death hadn't been in vain. Purdue wished he could have been here to see Genghis Khan's remains for himself, to be able to meet the man that fascinated him. That would have been amazing but unfortunately, that man never got to see his dreams fulfilled. Purdue had given him the hope that he might be part of finding the Great Khan's grave, but then that hope had been ripped away by whoever brought that blade down on his throat.

The others all climbed out of the hole they dug around the boulder and gathered nearby the bones. Purdue placed the skull on the ground above the rest of the bone formation that had been made. It was starting to resemble a human skeleton. Genghis Khan was laying on the ground in front of them, staring at them with his hollow eyes and his permanent smile. One of the most famous men in history had ended just like anyone else, nothing but bones—but it was him. It wasn't confirmed yet but Purdue could feel it. They had found Genghis Khan's tomb.

14

SETTLING OLD SCORES

The new Order of the Black Sun continued to dig up any stray remains that they found around the boulder, unearthing more and more pieces of the long dead world conqueror. When Purdue was satisfied by how much of him they found, and was sure that they weren't going to find much else in the ground, he scooped up all of the brittle old bones and put them in a large burlap sack he had brought to transport Genghis Khan's remains.

"We did it," Riley said with a broad grin. "We really found it."

"Because of you," Purdue said. "You brought that bow to my attention. That bow gave us what we needed to get here. We couldn't have done this without you, Miss Duda." He meant every word he said. She was still a novice to all of this but she had done well. She wrapped her arms around him and squeezed him into a hug. "You did good, lass. You did good."

The others looked pleased too. Despite the disastrous detours the journey had taken. Despite losing Shin Wo, who could have been a great help the rest of the way, they had navigated their way to the end of the quest and had found the treasure that they were hoping to find. Purdue hoped that Riley and especially Yusuke were seeing the value of being part of the Order of the Black Sun; that their membership made this all possible. They now had the resources to discover things that they may not have ever been able to uncover on their own. He hoped they left this expedition feeling fulfilled and satisfied with the group. And Purdue hoped that the rest of the order saw their success and realized that the Black Sun could be just as victorious with a guy like him in charge instead of a lunatic like Julian Corvus.

"So what now?" August asked.

Purdue looked out toward the edge of the plateau, toward the long drop that led back to the rest of the world below. The way up had been a challenge, and the descent might even be somehow worse. He shook his head. "I suppose we starting making our way down."

Everyone still looked happy with their success—but now a little less so.

The journey down the side of the plateau was almost just as difficult as the way up, but at least this time Purdue felt accomplished. The remains of Genghis Khan had been up there after all. There was no doubt anymore making him nervous for what was ahead. They had succeeded in everything they set out to do. That made the climb down a much more joyous event than it had been going the opposite direction. It also helped that there wasn't rain this time either.

Purdue had the sack of bones tightly secured around his back and it was odd knowing that he was carrying one of the most important figures of history like a backpack. Genghis Khan had probably never been carried by another person ever, probably not even when he was a baby. He probably emerged from the womb already full grown and a master warrior. Yet here Purdue was, lugging one of the most feared and respected leaders in all of mankind around on his bag. It was the most surreal piggyback ride Purdue had ever experienced. He knew he was the only one of the seven billion people on the planet that could say that they carried Genghis Khan down a mountain. The ancient warrior was a lot lighter now than he would have been in life.

The others all had smiles on their faces too, feeling just as accomplished. They should be smiling because Purdue knew he could have never done any of it without their help. They had all been great to work with in different ways, despite some of the tension between him and August that had transpired. When they got back into the city, they might go right back to that great hotel and have an even bigger meal than they did before.

It took a long while but they finally reached the bottom of the plateau, however, they weren't alone out there in the mountain range. Two silhouettes stood in front of them when they turned away from the rock face.

"We have really got to stop bumping into each other like this." Galen Fitzgerald was standing in a few feet away, looking giddy with excitement. "What you got there, Davy? You find Khan?"

Galen stood with Oniel at his side. Oniel stared at Purdue ravenously. Purdue knew those hollow eyes well. He had faced them down before. They were the eyes of a remorseless killer, who had zero qualms about gutting anyone that he felt like gutting. He knew firsthand how dangerous of a man Oniel was, and he knew that he was still probably a little upset with Purdue for killing his brother. Just like Galen, he had been part of the previous iteration of the Order of the Black Sun, just one of the many killers Julian Corvus had recruited and inserted into the order —something that Purdue was hoping to change. And also like Galen, Oniel couldn't have been pleased that Purdue had taken control of the Black Sun.

Two old enemies were standing in front of him, and they both wanted him dead. It was just as Galen had warned when those two enemies

stood outside with him in Mongolia. They were coming for him, it was just a matter of when and where. This was when and right beside that plateau was apparently where.

"You clever bastard," Galen snickered. "Are those them? Did you actually...Genghis Khan? If I'm being honest, I didn't think you would ever find those damn bones. Yet here you are. Of course, the great David Purdue never fails to get what he wants. Would you mind if I just stole a peak at them?"

Galen limped forward and Purdue backed away with the bag full of bones in hand. That step back cause Galen to break out into hysterics. He obviously thought it was a move of fear rather than just a simple step back from an enemy.

"Fine, Davy, you don't have to show me." Galen acted like he was performing for a loving crowd. "I just want to remind you that I warned you this was coming, didn't I? I said that we were going to settle our scores and here we are, to get everything in order."

"Oh, of course, Galen," Purdue said with an eye roll. "You just happen to have waited until I was done traversing Asia and climbing up and down this behemoth of a plateau. You were just standing by while we dragged our asses all over trying to find this. Wait until I'm tired as a goddamn dog and now you decide to take a shot at me."

"What are you implying?" Galen asked.

"Implying? No implication, you little shit. Just the truth. The truth is that you are coward and always have been. Hiding about until your opponent is running on fumes. Or worse! Stabbing an old man in his sleep. Sending mercenaries to take out people that you said you were going to come after yourself."

Galen raised a brow. "The hell you going on about? Mercenaries? Old men in their sleep?"

"Really, Galen?" Purdue couldn't help but laugh. He didn't know why Galen was still playing coy and not just reveling in his own actions like he usually did but it was annoying that he wasn't taking ownership of all of the horrible things he had done. "I'm going on about Shin Wo. Shin Wo. Ever heard of him?"

Galen threw his arms up in a dramatic shrug. "I can't say I have, no."

"We talked about him last time we were face to face. He had his throat slit in his tent."

"Oh, that's right," Galen said, clicking his tongue. "You did mention something about that before, didn't you? I still have no idea what you are talking about. That doesn't have anything to do with me at all."

"Well then Oniel did it!" Purdue roared.

Oniel stared at Purdue for a long moment and then shook his head. He couldn't voice a defense but the way he signaled his denial was powerful. He would have no reason to really lie about it so why were they? Or maybe they weren't...

Purdue kept pressing them. He had to. He needed to hear them admit to what they had done.

"Then you sent Wai Lin and her mercenaries after us a the Great Wall. Hate to tell you, but as you can see, you need to find better help."

Galen remained puzzled. "Wai Lin? Am I supposed to know that name too? You're throwing a whole lot of names at me, Davy boy, and you're really not making a lick of sense with any of them. Tell me a name I do know and then maybe then we can talk about them. Otherwise, I'm kind of left out here in the dark, my friend."

"You don't need to lie, Galen," Nina chimed in. "Why not just own up to what you've done."

"I would love to own up to it, but I'm still not even sure what it is I am supposed to have done here. None of this sounds familiar at all. Is this some kind of joke or what because I really don't get the punchline...kind of ruins the whole joke."

Purdue stepped forward, ready to rush Galen for acting so ignorant to his own crimes. He would probably be able to get a few good hits in before Oniel took him down. Maybe that would be worth it enough.

"Slow it down, Davy," Galen laughed uncomfortably. "I just came here to get some retribution on you. I didn't come here to be put on trial for things I had nothing to do with. Believe me, if I did have anything to do with them, you would have been the first to know."

Purdue had seen Galen lie. He had seen Galen put on an act to try and manipulate others. He had seen him fib and tell tall tales about his exploits. One thing that was universally accepted about that Irishman was that he was a terrible, terrible liar—and that's what made it clear that he wasn't lying.

"So you didn't kill Shin Wo...? Or send those hit men after us...?"

"Of course not," Galen said. "Why would I do that? Those things sound nothing like anything I would do. Really, Davy? You don't know me well at all."

Purdue thought back to those events, especially to their interrogation of Wai Lin. That mercenary hadn't been able to tell them much about her client. All she could really say was that he was a man who wanted to hurt Purdue. But she couldn't even tell him if the man who hired her was Irish or not...maybe he never was. There might have been someone else pulling the strings instead of it just being Galen. He had thought that the way those actions were being carried out didn't seem quite like Galen's usual M.O.

"None of it was you..."

"Not a single bit of it but I would love to hug whoever did to that you," Galen laughed venomously. "Look at you, they've done a lot more than just put you on edge with those stunts, haven't though? Damn, I wish I thought of something like that at one point. I could have had

PRESTON WILLIAM CHILD

so much more fun than we've had. Even now, my retribution isn't going to feel quite as sweet now."

"But...but..."

Purdue's mind was racing again. With how exhausted he was from the lack of sleep in recent nights and from the climb up to and down from the tomb, he could barely stand and now this revelation was completely rocking his head. There was no way that Galen was innocent of all of it, yet, here he was and Purdue really believed him. Him showing up the morning of Shin Wo's death, minutes after Purdue discovered his body was what then? A coincidence? And who was Wai Lin's client if not Galen!?

"You aren't working with August either?"

"Can you drop that already?" August asked irritably. "I told you, I can't stand this prick."

Galen pointed his cane at August. "I don't know either of those names you asked me about...but him...him I know. Yeah, you, I know you! Yes, I'd recognize a great big titan like you anywhere. From back with the Order of the Black Sun. You were always stomping around. Gus, eh?"

"August." The big man scowled when he corrected him, looking ready to tear Galen in half.

"August!" Galen laughed. "Yes, that's it. So you've decided to keep serving the new regime, is that it?"

"I like a steady paycheck. A solid job. Why

lose all of that just to throw a temper tantrum for not getting what you wanted?"

Purdue watched the interaction closely and listened to every word that pass between the two men. He still wasn't completely convinced that August and Julian weren't in some clandestine alliance. This could all just be an act to try and throw off suspicion.

Galen continued to speak to August with his trademark taunts. "As I recall, you were something of a bruiser, eh? One of those tough, red-knuckled bastards weren't you? You're the one who threw a lad right through a wall at the compound once, weren't you?"

"I was," August said. "He deserved it."

"You love getting into a good scrap. I've always been more a fan of observing a fight. A spectator. Fun to watch and you get hurt far less from the sidelines. But let me tell you, my friend here loves to fight too. You know him too right? From back in the order?"

August glanced to Oniel. "The mute. I remember him."

"Exactly," Galen snickered. "He's not much of a talker but he makes up for that with his love of throwing around some violence. He's a fighter like you. Isn't that right, Davy? Oniel loves a fight!"

"He loves murdering innocent people, yes," Purdue said, having seen the depths of Oniel's depravity on a misguided treasure hunt some time back. "A real good fighter. Killing people in their sleep."

"So what do you say, Davy? What say we place some bets? You brought your fighter. I brought mine. Winner gets the Khan's bones. Seems only fitting. Inflicting some violence to honor one of the most violent men to ever walk the Earth?"

Purdue practically hugged the bag in his arms. "That is not going to happen. Why the hell would we go along with some gamble like that?"

Galen reached around and pulled a pistol from his belt. "Easy answer...you don't actually have a choice. Now stop having such poor form. There's nothing better than a good bet. Let's settle our feud once and for all. One on one. You against me."

"If that was the case, you and I would be throwing punches...not them."

"Oh grow up, Davy," Galen laughed. "Rich men like us don't usually get our hands dirty with the fighting. We have others do that for us. It's just how the world works."

"I've got this," August said beside Purdue. He turned to see August and the man towered over him, looking ready and willing for the fight. Purdue still wasn't even sure if he could trust him, or if this was just another part of an act; nothing more than some sick joke that Galen was playing on him. He looked back at the others who all looked worried but unsure of how to proceed. August put his big hand on his shoulder and repeated his words. "I've got this. Trust me."

The pair of men approached one another and the difference between the two opponents physically was startling. August was a massive, tank of a man with broad shoulders and muscular arms. Oniel, by contrast, was tall and lanky, barely a stick of a man but Purdue knew not to underestimate him. He and his late twin brother, Alton, had both been that way but had still become the most dangerous killers in Jamaica. He knew that August was tough but he would really have to fight well to beat someone like Oniel.

"You weren't around the order long," August said to Oniel tauntingly. "But I've got to say, you left an impression, man. You creeped me out each and every time I saw you in the halls. Just staring. Always staring. Scary stuff. Was always hoping I'd get the chance to get you to stop creeping people out."

Oniel naturally didn't respond but his usual hollow stare had a glimmer of excitement in it. He was apparently looking forward to shutting August up. Or maybe he was just anxious to get him out of the way so he could go after his real target, Purdue.

While watching, a small part of Purdue was still nervous that this was all an act and August was just making it look convincing. But then the other part of him really wanted to cheer August on and root for him to kick the hell out of Oniel. He would prefer for this whole sick gladiatorial battle to not even happen but Galen's firearm was making the decision. If they didn't go along with it, then they could all be gunned down pretty quick. It was a typical Galen Fitzgerald move to just force his way into getting his way. He was like a small little boy throwing a tantrum, but instead of throwing toys, he would be throwing bullets at a very high velocity.

August tried to use his overwhelming size to take an early advantage in the fight but Oniel was nimble and agility was incredible. He sidestepped August like a matador facing a bull and caused August to go stumbling straight past him and crashing down to the rocks. In those seconds that August was down, Oniel stared at Purdue like he was thinking about taking those fleeting moments to end him quick before August recovered. Purdue tried to brace himself but he knew he couldn't beat Oniel. He wouldn't even be able to protect himself for very long at all. He had barely managed to beat Oniel's twin brother and that was mostly thanks to the element of surprise and having a sword in his hand. Not to mention, Oniel was always the more dangerous of the two murderous brothers.

Thanks to August though, Purdue didn't have to try and hold off the mute assailant. August got back to his feet quickly and went at Oniel full throttle again. This time, the two grappled and despite August's superior strength, Oniel was taking opportunities to go after weak points, going for his throat and his eyes. It was a dirty way to fight but there weren't exactly rules when it came to fights out in the wilderness, where the ring was nothing more than a series of rocks.

Purdue hoped that August would be able to just barrel his way and end this fight early, maybe push Oniel off a cliff like he had pushed that man off of the Great Wall of China. Unfortunately, this wasn't going to be nearly as easy as he wished it would be.

Galen watched the fight with wide, excited eyes and with his mouth hanging open. He reminded Purdue of a little boy sitting on the floor enjoying his favorite show like it was the only thing in the entire universe that mattered or even existed. Galen seemed to especially love the fact that it seemed like his fighter had the upper hand. Oniel was fighting like a wild animal. His movements were unpredictable but weren't erratic. They were precise blows. There was some kind of method to all of the madness, that was for sure.

August tried his best to defend himself from the onslaught but he wasn't faring very well. His size was helpful when it came to enduring the attacks but he could only do that for so long. At some point, Oniel was going to manage to break through and probably cause some real damage.

Purdue wanted to focus on the fight but all he

could think about was the strange circumstances surrounding all of this. Something was amiss about this entire venture, and surprisingly Galen wasn't the cause of whatever strange feeling he was having.

"So you really didn't do any of it?" Purdue called over to Galen, ignoring the fight.

Galen seemed annoyed to have to take his attention away from the brawl and shook his head. "None of it, Davy. It was brilliant work though. Cracked your head and turned you paranoid better than I ever could have. They really deserve a round of applause."

"Then something is going on here, Galen. Someone is messing with us."

"Messing with you, you mean."

"No, with us!" Purdue said. "You included."

Galen's eyes kept darting from the fight and then back to Purdue with some annoyance like Purdue was the worst distraction that he had ever had to deal with. As he started to think about it though, the Irishman started watching the brawl less and less.

"How do you figure that, eh?"

"You really think they didn't know that I would blame you for all of it? Hell, they practically framed you."

"And how could this mysterious person know so much about any of it?" Galen asked with little concern. Purdue reached into his jacket pocket and Galen aimed his pistol at him threateningly.

"Oi! The hell you think you are doing, Purdue? Drop that shit now!"

Purdue slowly and cautiously pulled out the thin stack of pictures that Wai Lin had been given by her client; the snapshots of Purdue from all different points in time.

"Is this some goddamn distraction tactic, Davy? I said drop that shit now!"

"I am!" Purdue yelled back, tossing the pictures at Galen's feet and then putting his hands up in surrender. "Look! Look at those pictures, Galen."

Galen carefully glanced down at the photographs by his feet, but still kept his gun trained on Purdue. He examined them as best as he could while also making sure his enemies were in his sights and shook his head.

"So someone likes taking pictures of you...what's the big deal?"

"The big deal, Galen, is that I thought that you had taken those pictures."

"Why the hell would I get myself a photo album of you?"

"Some of those pictures are from after my house burned, when you and Julian took all my things and took all my money, remember? When you thought I was dead."

Galen flashed a broad grin. "Aw, yes. Some of the best months of my life. What sweet memories. I wish we could go back to that time."

"My point is...is that you didn't know I was

alive during that. You thought I died in that house fire just like Julian Corvus did, just like Nina did, just like everyone did. You had no idea that I managed to get out of there in time."

"Course I didn't," Galen said. "If I had, I would have hunted your cockroach ass down."

Purdue's head was still spinning with all of this information. Galen really was innocent of all of the bad shit that had happened on this venture. He was here now to cause trouble sure, but like usual, he wasn't really much of a threat. There really was someone else out there, someone much worse that hadn't shown themselves, at least not yet.

August and Oniel were still trading hard blows in their fight. They were both battered and bloody. Oniel in particular looked like he was barely standing, and was staring at August with those hateful orbs in his eyes sockets. He wasn't like Galen. He didn't give a damn about sportsmanship or any sort of fair fight. The one thing Purdue always thought of when he thought about Oniel and his late twin brother were the knives they kept in their sleeves for when they decided to do their killing, and sure enough, Oniel suddenly reached into his sleeve and unveiled a blade.

"Hey!" Yusuke yelled, pointing at Oniel. "That wasn't part of the deal!"

Galen didn't seem to care. He was still only half paying attention. The rest of his attention belonged to the pictures at his feet as he considered Purdue's words.

Oniel lunged at August and August managed to grab hold of his wrist, stopping the blade from getting closer. Oniel pushed forward and tried to get the knife into August's body. It was a struggle where if August slipped up for even a second, those five inches of metal were going to be inside of his face.

Purdue was about to intervene when something moved by him in the other direction. Nina sprinted at Galen out of nowhere, before Galen could even fully process what was happening. She ripped the gun out of the Irishman's hand and pistol whipped him onto the ground. It wasn't the first time Purdue had seen her with a firearm but he was always impressed with just how capable she was in a fight if it got serious.

Nina aimed the pistol and fired one shot into Oniel's back. The Jamaican man stopped his assault and staggered backward a few steps, turning around to face Nina. That bullet must have hurt but Oniel, as usual, didn't show his emotions very clearly on his face. He took a step toward her and sneered. He probably would have spoken some foul language if he was able to. Nina pulled the trigger again and again as Oniel started to approach. One bullet grazed his arm, the other planted itself in his stomach. He was still coming though, with those hollow eyes and his knife rising in his hand.

Nina let out a yell and pulled the trigger over and over again. Each bullet ripped through Oniel as he approached. He was close enough to maybe swipe at her with his blade when the last bullet plunged into the center of his skull and he dropped the ground dead at Nina's feet, his body riddled with bullets. Nina was still trying to pull the trigger, just out of pure survival instinct, but it clicked harmlessly as it was out of bullets. She was breathing heavily and her teeth were chattering.

When she finally caught her breath, she kicked at Oniel's body to make sure he was dead and then turned to Purdue angrily. "I don't know what exactly made you cross paths with a guy like this or what you did to get on his bad side but if I had been there and not been a prisoner when you met this psycho, I would have told you to not go anywhere near someone like him!"

Everyone stood in shock at her sudden display of brutal heroism. August got to his feet and thanked her for saving his life while Yusuke and Riley could just watch the whole thing with flabbergasted expressions.

Galen was getting up from the ground, his brow bleeding from where he had been hit with the gun. He tried to reach for Oniel's blade that had rolled toward him but Nina stomped on his hand when he tried, pointing the gun at him.

Galen winced from the pain in his hand but then started laughing as he looked down the barrel of the gun.

"I forgot just how ferocious you could be, Dr. Gould," Galen laughed, looking up at her. "But you do realize that you're out of bullets, eh?"

"I do, yes," Nina said darkly. She raised the gun over her head like she was about to use it as a club if Galen dared make a move. "There are other ways to use a firearm."

Purdue was honestly relieved that Oniel was dead. Of all of the many enemies he had made over the course of his career, Oniel was one of the scariest. He wasn't someone that could be reasoned with or negotiated with. He was just silent death, stalking toward his victims. The last remnant of the Wharf Man and his defunct crime ring that had given Purdue so much trouble at one point. And now Galen was beaten too.

Things really were looking up.

15

P urdue held the sack of bones in his hand tightly. He and his team had gotten their prize and gotten rid of some of their most frequent obstacles. Galen and Oniel were threats to the new roster of the Black Sun, still holding onto old grudges. There were a few holdover issues that Purdue wanted to tidy up when he took over the Order of the Black Sun. Galen and Oniel were one of those issues. There were going to have to be dealt with at one point or another, especially given that their issues were very personally with Purdue, and not even just the order as a whole.

"So I think that means you've won the game, Davy," Galen said, still pinned to the ground by Nina's foot. "Or, I should say...Dr. Gould won the game for you. We had you, you know."

"Sure, Galen," Purdue said with an eye roll.

"You would have gotten away with it if not for us meddling kids and all that shit."

"So, we're going to kill him, right?" Nina asked, still standing on Galen. They had talked about having to put Galen and Oniel down but now that Purdue knew that Galen wasn't responsible for Shin Wo's death, it didn't seem quite as necessary to do that. Then again, he was always going to be a threat. The man never knew when to give up or toss aside old grudges. There was no purging the bad blood between them, at least not easily. "As discussed?"

"N-n-no," Galen muttered, his eyes widening. He turned to Purdue pleadingly. "Davy, you can't! That's not what you do!"

"Maybe not what I usually do, no," Purdue said with a shrug. "But you just watched Nina unload a whole clip into Oniel. She barely even knew Oniel...but you...you made her time as a prisoner pretty miserable didn't you? You think she's going to hesitate putting you down?"

"I won't," Nina said just for emphasis and holding the pistol over her head, ready to bring it down on Galen's skull.

"Or maybe we should let August do it," Purdue said, giving August a pat on the back. August glanced to him with uncertainty but Purdue just smiled. It was nice knowing that he and Galen weren't in league after all. "You did sick your beast on him just a few minutes ago. Plus, I just don't think he likes you, aye?"

"Never have," August confirmed.

Galen was practically a blubbering mess on the ground. He was never the most dignified man but especially not when he was backed into a corner with very little chance of escaping. He would break down as much as he needed to if it meant gaining any sort of sympathy or even pity, anything that would keep him alive.

"Davy! Please! I didn't do those things you accused me of! None of it!"

"Aye, maybe not," Purdue admitted. "But you've done plenty of bad, Galen. Plenty of it. And don't like you haven't. We both know the truth."

"I can change!"

"Highly doubt it," Nina said sternly.

Purdue walked up beside Nina, looking down at Galen. He had initially just been a colleague, someone he only ever saw at fundraisers or parties. They had then become sort of friendly rivals, at least from Galen's perspective, but Purdue never liked him very much. And because of Galen's insecurities, he had made Purdue into an enemy.

"Davy!" Galen cried out.

Purdue and Galen locked eyes and he saw just how broken this fragile man was now. He had propped himself up with so many attempts to seem powerful and all of them had come crumbling down. He quit the Order of the Black Sun and now he lost his best friend. He was pretty powerless now, just back to the same old pitiful Galen that Purdue always knew; the one trying so hard to make himself seem bigger than he was.

"Fine," Purdue said.

Before a debate of any kind could break out, something sounded out nearby.

There was a slight rumbling in the air before a helicopter curved around a cliff into view. Its propeller cut through the air threateningly as the chopper approached them. They all stared up at it but with the sun behind the chopper, there was a disorienting glare when they tried to make out more about it.

Purdue held the bag of bones even tighter in his grasp. Whatever this was, it couldn't be good.

The helicopter slowly landed, sending of the surrounding grass into disarray. Once it touched down, a man hopped out and began walking toward them. His trench coat and dirty blond hair whipped around him in the helicopter's windstorm but he was steady as he moved. Once he was close, he gave a half-hearted smile, pointing at the sack of bones in Purdue's hand.

"You found them? Wonderful. I'll be taking those off of your hands then."

Purdue laughed but part of him was shaking with anxiousness. He had no idea who this was and how he knew what they came for...but however he did, there was something dangerous about him. Maybe he was a friend of Galen's but when Purdue looked in Galen's direction, the Irishman seemed just as baffled by the stranger as he was.

"That's not going to happen," Purdue said. "You should at least buy me dinner first."

The man looked at him and frowned. "Really? You? You're the guy?"

"The guy?"

"The new guy," the man sighed. "The new boss of the Black Sun. That couldn't possibly be you." He rubbed his face with disappointment. "Oh it is...that's...ugh. I'm sorry, I don't mean to be rude. I just expected that whoever was running the Black Sun now would be...someone with a bit more presence. I doubt I'll remember you in a couple hours."

He knew quite a lot about the Order of the Black Sun for a complete stranger.

"And just who the hell might you be, aye?"

The man raised his arms in the air and shrugged. "Me? I'm nobody."

"You know a lot for someone who is a nobody."

The man smiled again and then held out his hand expectantly, gesturing toward the bag in Purdue's grasp. "You can hand over Khan or I could kill every last one of you and take him myself."

"Now just hold on a minute!" Nina broke in, raising her hands. "This is ridiculous. You could at least tell us who you are before you start spewing out demands and threats."

The man just kept smiling. "Sorry if I seem crass...I'm not much of a talker."

Purdue hadn't felt so nervous since the first time he met Julian Corvus. This man had a similar way about him—like a volcano on the verge of eruption. Somehow Purdue believed that this man would absolutely make good on his threats. It wasn't just empty talk unfortunately.

"Last chance."

His pithy negotiation tactics felt like a countdown on a bomb. It was ticking down, and getting very close to zero. Any minute now, they would have to deal with that explosion.

When no one made a move, the man chuckled to himself again. "You really have no idea, do you? You mean to tell me that you had no idea what you were signing up for when you took your new job. That's not good...incompetent really Are you sure that you were the right choice for your position? I've been watching you fumble around every step of the way."

"You've been watching us? For how long?"

"Long enough to figure out what kind of man the great David Purdue really is...and you're a mess of a man. A real bad mess. You didn't respond too well to any of the things I put in your way."

A thought dawned on Purdue and he immediately knew it was true.

"It was you. You killed Shin Wo."

"I did, yes. He was far too helpful to you." The man showed no remorse during his confession. "And rather than think it over, you jumped straight to accusing your friends and allies of the deed. How pathetic. Just another example of your ineptitude."

"It wasn't just what happened with Shin Wo." Purdue was starting to put the pieces together and finally things were starting to make some sense. Everything that had happened seemed clearer than ever before. "It was much more than that, aye? All of this. It was all of it. You did it."

"Yes," the man said plainly. "Right from the very beginning." He glanced at Riley. "Did you really think that she stumbled upon a random bow that gave such a big clue for finding the location of the tomb? Really? Do clues like that usually manifest themselves so easily? Of course not."

Riley's face was growing red and she even seemed to be biting back tears. Purdue wanted to tell her it was okay but he couldn't find the words. She stuttered, trying to speak up for herself. "I thought I..."

"Found something amazing?" The man cut her off with a chuckle. "Sure, lady, but only because I served it up to you on a silver platter; only because I allowed you to find it. The tomb of Genghis Khan...lost for centuries...it all sounds so tempting doesn't it? Too enticing for

David Purdue and his new Order of the Black Sun to pass up, wasn't it? And so, like moths to a bug zapper, you went racing toward it with evidence that should have been suspect from the start. I thought it was too obvious, that someone with your reputation would figure it out. But you didn't. Didn't you ever wonder why the tomb of Genghis Khan had never been found after hundreds of years of digs and excavations? Especially now? With all of the advanced tech we have out in the world? We because it already was. We found it years ago. You can't discover what's already been discovered."

Purdue looked at the sack full of bones in his hand and found himself questioning just how real any of this was. Was he just holding glorified props, put in place to make him feel accomplished? Was this all just part of the show?

"Oh, don't worry," the man said reassuringly. "Those are the real deal. And that was indeed the real tomb. It's just that we put everything back where it belonged for you to find it."

"Why?" Purdue couldn't fathom the answer. It all seemed like so much effort just to mess with him.

"For this to work, we needed everything to be as real as possible. Real, accurate locations. Real bones. All we had to do was leave obvious breadcrumbs about for you to follow. To be frank, it was a hell of a lot harder for us. We didn't have someone pointing in the right direction. You're welcome, by the way."

Purdue couldn't believe what he was hearing. There was no way this could have all been so carefully orchestrated by an outside force. There were too many factors...too many variables and little details to control for this to be true.

"So you're trying to tell me that this was all...what? Some bloody test?"

"Exactly," the man smirked. "You all were just running through the mouse tubes that we built, trying so hard to get to that cheese that we put in the cage. We needed to see how the new Order of the Black Sun would do. So we gave you a quest and then threw all kinds of obstacles in your path to see how you would do."

"Like killing Shin Wo," Yusuke said, looking furious but nodding begrudgingly, understanding just how intense of a situation they were in.

"Yes," the man said. "Like I said, he was too helpful. He was contaminating the test results. To get the best understanding of how you operated, we needed to take someone like that off of the board. We needed to see how you would react to all kinds of situations. Like sending Wai Lin to see how you would handle a sudden ambush in a public setting."

This was indeed the man who had hired her and her mercenaries, after all.

"Or making it look like one of your old

enemies was far greater of a threat than he actually was."

Purdue felt like a puppet. He could practically see the strings hanging from his joints. He had been played. They all had been played. And the worst part was that he didn't even know who these puppeteers even were. At least when he was fighting Julian Corvus, he knew his enemy. Even this man in front of him, this grand manipulator that had spun him up like a wind-up doll, was still nameless.

Galen limped forward. His face still looked horrible from the scuffle. Purdue expected Galen to take a place beside the new arrival. They could have been working together after all...then again, this didn't feel like Galen's style. This man was taking all of the glory from anyone else by being so in control. There was no way Galen would allow that to happen. And he'd also framed Galen as well which wasn't a great thing to do to someone. Sure enough, Galen didn't seem to be a big fan of this man—something that he and Purdue could finally agree on.

"Looks like we have got ourselves some big time puppet master, eh? You like stringing us all along, eh? Mr. Pied Piper and you're just leading us all to where you would like us to go. Look at you. You love having that power. You love being in charge...but this doesn't concern you. All of this is between the Order of the Black Sun and people like me...that used to be part of it. So unless you have a membership in the order before Davy's time and before my time with the Black Sun, then why don't you make like a tree...and get the hell out of here, eh?"

Galen's pompous nature was usually insufferable but right now Purdue appreciated Galen's aggressive negotiation tactics. It probably wasn't a smart time to use them, but he had to admire the Irishman's brashness. Hopefully it was enough to get this man to back down but Purdue doubted it, especially when that man just started smiling.

"I'm sorry," the man said. "Who are you?"

That was the biggest insult anyone could ever give Galen. He loved recognition, he loved fame, and he loved being respected. Not being recognized was like a physical blow to a narcissistic man like that. His face grew red and he looked ready to start swinging his cane around and beat this newcomer to death. He bit back on that anger, squeezed his walking stick tightly and just chuckled instead.

"My name is Galen Fitzgerald," Galen said, and then waited a moment, like he expected the name to get a reaction. It didn't. The man just looked at him blankly. "Perhaps you have read my book. I'm just as world renowned as Davy and if this is about the Black Sun...well, I'm no longer with them but I was for longer than Purdue has been..."

"Why should I care about any of this?" The

man said with a smile and looked right past Galen, like he was nothing more than a wall in his way. He craned his head around Galen and spoke to Purdue again. "Give me the bones, Purdue. Now."

Galen was seething from being ignored and he moved to strike the man with his cane but the man caught the stick before it ever reached him. He looked at Galen with some pity like the Irishman was just a kid playing around with toys.

"Listen, you're not nearly as important as you think you are," the man said coldly. "The business going on here is between my superiors, who I represent, and the Order of the Black Sun. In your own words, you said you are no longer part of their order. So, it looks to me, Mr. Leprechaun that you're the one who should...how did you put it? Make like a tree...and get the hell out of here..."

The man suddenly drew his pistol and pulled the trigger. A bullet plunged into Galen's chest and he staggered away a few steps before collapsing onto his back. Blood spread across his lower torso, right over his stomach. It was a bad wound, but one that would take some time to kill him. Galen yelled from the pain and Purdue's team all froze, knowing that they probably shouldn't try and face the person with a loaded gun, especially someone who they didn't know well. He could be capable of anything, maybe even killing all of them.

"I really had no intention of killing Fitzgerald. I forgot he might even be here to be honest. He was good to have to throw you off our scent but now...now that you know we exist...there's not all that much use for him now. This might have even been for the best." The man spoke about shooting Galen like he was trying to figure out if he had ordered the right food for lunch. "Notice how no one's rushing to help you, Galen. That's a bit pathetic, isn't it? You obviously weren't great at making friends."

The man lowered his gun and then took a step forward toward the group.

"Now, Purdue," the man held out his free hand. "Give me the bones back and we can continue this conversation."

Purdue glanced to his team. They all looked understandably uneasy considering the situation they had been thrust into. Purdue didn't think they would have to deal with someone as dangerous as Julian Corvus anytime soon but this unnamed newcomer was on that same level. One move that annoyed him, and who knew who would drop next. They had to be very with this—and more importantly, they needed to get away from this man.

Purdue took a step forward with the bag of bones. The late, great, world conqueror jingled in his hands as he stepped toward the man. The man looked pleased by Purdue's surrender but Purdue really had no intention of giving over his prize—at least not the way that this man wanted.

Purdue tightened his grip on the burlap sack and swung the bag as hard as he could. The bones inside jangled as they collided into the man's face. He hoped that some of those bones were sharp enough to draw some blood. The man crashed onto his back, completely knocked off balance by the bag of bones. Genghis Khan had probably hurt a lot of people back in his day, but not quite like that. He could have kept beating the man but he knew that the man's men in the helicopter wouldn't sit back and watch. Escape was more important in this instance than trying to win a fight.

The rest of the team all looked stunned by Purdue and he motioned them all to start running. There was a chance to get away if they could lose their pursuers through the mountains. There were cliffs and caves in the mountain range but also many areas thick with trees and woodlands. That would be their best bet to get out of sight, anywhere that they could hide from the helicopter that was no doubt already being prepared for pursuit.

Purdue held the bag of bones in one hand and then heaved the wounded Galen up to his feet with the other. He slung Galen's arm over his shoulder and the Irishman yelped in pain as he was being moved. It was probably better for him to stay laying down but that wasn't really an option. Purdue could have just left him behind—Galen certainly would have left him to die—but Purdue wasn't Galen. He didn't care how terrible Galen was. He wasn't just going to abandon him as he was bleeding out. If there was a chance to save his life—as pathetic of a life as it was—then he would take it.

Everyone hurried as quickly as they could as they ran into a forested area, covered by a thick layer of branches and leaves, hoping it would be enough cover to lose the chopper, if only for a moment or two.

"Who the hell...was that...?" Galen muttered beside Purdue as Purdue tried to go as fast as he could with the near-dead wight clinging to him. "That...bastard shot me."

The trees moved as a sudden windstorm swept over them. They could hear the helicopter blades twirling through the sky as the aircraft moved over the forest. They all kept still and low, doing their best not to be seen by their pursuers.

That man's voice rang out over the trees. It sounded like he was on a megaphone and the helicopter itself might have been rigged with speakers. "Not that I'm not having fun, but if you could all do me a favor and come on out, I would really appreciate it! Otherwise, we're going to have to come storming in after you. That could be a lot of fun for us but I imagine it will be a lot less fun for you!"

The message grew louder as he passed

overhead and then grew feint as the helicopter soared over another part of the forest. It started doing circles, arching back around, and the man continued to deliver all of kinds of messages.

"If you come out, I'll tell you my name. Doesn't that sound like a good deal to you, David Purdue?"

"Don't make me turn this into Vietnam. We've got napalm stocked up in here. I don't mind setting this whole place on fire if it means flushing you out!"

The man was circling above them like a bird of prey. They knew that the second he caught sight of them, he would dive bomb and snatch up their lives like they were nothing more than little mice. They were severely outgunned by that chopper. They wouldn't last long if they exposed themselves, but things had reached a stalemate—and that stalemate would have to break one way or another.

16

THE FIVE-LEAF CLOVER

G alen Fitzgerald wasn't looking good at all but still managed to weakly offer a suggestion beside Purdue. "Maybe...maybe it would be best if you just gave up and give him the bones...call it a day."

"Right, like that would be enough to satiate him. I know his type. He is the same class of bastard as Julian was. He'll still kill us all if we do that. Besides, you just want to see us lose, don't you?

Galen managed a pained chuckle. He was looking worse and worse by the second. "You're not...you're not entirely wrong, Davy. I have to admit...it would be nice to really see you lose...especially...especially if these are my last few moments on Earth. Hell...let's just consider it my...final request..."

Purdue couldn't believe Galen was trying to

pull that card. "I'm not doing that and got to hell with your last wishes. We'll find another way."

"It's your funeral then," Galen said. "At least...at least I won't die alone then...I appreciate that. I knew we were friends..."

"We're not friends."

"You keep telling yourself that. It's why you couldn't...couldn't bring yourself to let Dr. Gould kill me. I saw...I saw what happened just before that helicopter showed up. You were going to tell her to let me live..."

Purdue had kind of hoped Galen hadn't seen that, but it had nothing to do with them being friends. It had more to do with Galen not wanting to get blood on their hands if they didn't have to. They had neutralized Galen at the time. It might have been a bad decision, but it was the one he had chosen.

"See? We're too close of mates. We piss each other off now and then but in the end, we're practically brothers..."

Now he was just getting ridiculous.

"You are definitely losing too much blood. It's starting to affect your brain."

The helicopter passed by overhead. Everyone looked so nervous, like they were stuck with no way out. That couldn't have been true. In Purdue's experience, there was always something that could be done. They just needed time to think of one.

"Let's keep moving," he suggested. "We'll figure something out, aye?"

None of them looked like they shared his optimism. This was a new kind of opponent. He had been practically invisible until that helicopter landed, stealthily influencing so much of this expedition without them realizing he was even there. How were they supposed to fight someone like that? It would be especially hard now that he switched from sabotage to assault and had the firepower to kill them if he had the chance.

Purdue ignored the worried expressions and motioned them forward. He still had to be at the back of the pack since he was dragging Galen at his side. Galen seemed like he was barely even trying to help him with their movement. Purdue would usually be annoyed by Galen moaning and groaning, but he made an exception for the bullet in the Irishman's stomach. This was one time where he didn't blame Galen for whining. It was bad and they didn't exactly have the proper medical tools to tend to his injury, especially right now, running for their lives.

They needed to get away from the helicopter, and lugging a wounded man was slowing them down. Part of Purdue wanted to just drop Galen like dead weight and leave that bastard behind, but he couldn't go through with that. He couldn't stand him but Galen hadn't always been an enemy. There was a time not long ago when

Galen Fitzgerald was just an obnoxious colleague. And as much as Purdue didn't like him —especially after Galen's multiple attempts to kill him—he didn't like seeing Galen had such a slow, and painful death.

Purdue could feel Galen slowing down beside him. "Davy...put me...put me down...you bastard...put me down..."

Purdue glanced to his left and saw Galen's head bowed low, his face a ghostly shade of white. He was fading quickly, only hanging on by the end of a very thin thread of life.

Purdue gently lowered Galen down so he leaned against the trunk of a tree. Galen just sat there, pale and dazed, but hands cupping the hole in his belly. There was blood all over him. He looked up at Purdue with an expression that Purdue had never seen him make before —remorse.

Galen coughed but even his cough was weak and strained. "This is a wee bit of a problem that we find ourselves in, eh?" Galen licked some speckles of blood off of his lip. "Truth be told, it hurts...it hurts like hell...you ever have a bullet in your gut?"

"I've taken a bullet or two in my day, aye," Purdue said honestly. "Some blades too. I've been run through by worse things than that bullet too."

Galen smirked, like he took that as Purdue trying to be better than him. "And how...and how did you manage to keep on ticking? The cogs in my clock seem to be a bit broken, I'm afraid."

"Well, the Holy Grail saved me once."

That wasn't a great memory for Purdue. He'd spent most of it on the verge of death and only been saved thanks to the efforts of his friends and that blessed cup. It was one of the closer calls when it came to the end of his mortal life.

"You wouldn't happen to have that in your bag, would you?"

"I'm afraid not."

"I'll make do with a Guinness then."

"Sorry," Purdue couldn't help but smile a little. "I'm not carrying one of those around either. I prefer sobriety when I'm doing something important like this."

Galen balked. "That's part of what made you such a goddamn bore, Davy." Galen looked down and his eyes seemed to be struggling to even look at his surroundings. "Aw well, you wouldn't have given me it either way, would you?"

"Of course I would have."

Galen looked genuinely surprised. He bit back whatever little jabs that he was about to say. There were no cheeky or pithy retorts from him for once. He was utterly taken aback by that. Maybe Purdue was finally getting through to Galen about the truth. But just in case he wasn't, he decided to spell it out for him.

"I'm not the piece of shit that you seem to have painted me as in your head. I'm not trying to ruin your life or your career or any of the other shit you have accused me of. I never was, you loon."

Galen managed a blood-filled smile. "Perhaps I was a wee bit dramatic. But you are a stubborn, smug bastard, you know that?"

"Look who is talking."

Galen winced and his breathing slowed.

"I'm going to tell you something, Davy. I don't tell people this. I never have but if I'm really going to die in this shit place, I might as well say as much as I can, eh? So here it is." Galen paused for a moment, like he was reconsidering his decision, but then he pressed on. "I have always tried to find four leaf clovers on my property before I'd go travel. It didn't matter where I was going, I always just wanted to have a little bit of luck on my side, you understand? Am I a stereotypical Irishman for doing such a thing? Aye. I may be. But..." Galen groaned and the muscles in his face flinched. "But the last time I did it...it was right before I followed you to Mongolia." Galen's voice grew quieter and weaker with word that left his mouth. "I didn't find any four leaves that mourning. Not a single one."

It was a bit of a pathetic story but that usually wouldn't affect Purdue much. However, seeing someone who was usually so full of himself like Galen in such a vulnerable place somehow made it very difficult to hear.

Purdue shook his head but presented a smile. "So you should have realized that this wasn't ever going to be a lucky trip for you then."

Galen gave a pained giggle.

"That's the thing, Davy. I didn't find a four leaf clover...but I found one with five leaves. Five. It was the first time ever...tell me...tell me, what the hell does a five leaf clover even mean? What kind of fortune am I...am I supposed to get from five leaves?"

"I'm not sure," Purdue said truthfully. He tried to look positive but he could practically see the life escaping through every pore of Galen's body. "But given your current situation, I don't think it meant anything good."

"Evidently not."

Galen looked sadder than Purdue had ever seen him. He was so used to seeing the Irishman either look so smug and proud of himself, or red-faced and furious with anger. Seeing him look so full of regret and sorrow was strange. It hardly even looked like Galen Fitzgerald at all anymore.

"It looks like..." Galen struggled to speak and his eyes froze in their sockets, his gaze fixated on Purdue. "Looks like you won in the end, Davy."

That cheeky, petty, and envious light behind the Irishman's eyes went out. Galen's lifeless stare remained on Purdue. His attention was drawn on Purdue just as it had always been, trying so hard to be him, or to surpass him.

In another life, one where Galen wasn't

narcissistic, violent, and annoying, the two rich men might have even been friends. They had similar interest and worked in similar circles but their personalities were far too distinct from one another. They were always going to have clashed in those conditions, and they had many times.

Mostly, Purdue felt pity for the man. Galen had wasted so much of his life trying to prove himself to everyone else, even going to such hostile lengths to do it. Had he been less insecure and more comfortable with who he was, he may not have ever ended up in such a bad situation. IF he had spent less time blaming others for his misfortune, maybe there could have been a chance for him.

"Purdue."

He drew his attention away from the corpse against the tree and found Nina standing nearby, having apparently come back to check on him. She looked from him to the dead body beside him and her eyes grew wide but eh could see the conflict on her face. There was no real sadness there.

"Is he...?"

"Gone," Purdue said, gently brushing his hand over Galen's face to close his eye lids. "Aye."

Nina didn't look at all upset and he couldn't blame her. Galen had been a part of the Black Sun when they had held her prisoner for months. According to her, he hadn't just gone along with it like some bystander, but had relished every moment of her imprisonment. She wouldn't be shedding any tears for someone like that, and neither would Purdue.

Although he and Galen had shared a brief moment of peace and understanding at the end, Galen was not a friend. His attempts to kill Purdue wouldn't just suddenly be forgotten or not matter. No, he wouldn't mourn Galen Fitzgerald just like he wouldn't mourn Oniel. They were bad guys and threats to Purdue's life. They probably deserved the horrible ends that they got.

Purdue could hear helicopter blades over the trees coming back in their general direction. Nina heard it too and stared up with worry. That man was getting closer.

Purdue looked at Galen's body and considered trying to cat him out of there on his back but there was no way he could do that. He was already carrying one dead man. A fresh carcass was going to be a lot heavier than the literal bag of bones that used to be Genghis Khan.

The only choice was to leave him behind. Purdue gave his old wannabe-rival one last look. At least, he had died in a relatively peaceful place. Given the dangerous life Galen lived and the bad company he kept, he could have died cut into little pieces or blown up. He may have gone out bloody, but he was relatively whole.

Purdue picked up Galen's cane and he and

Nina started running in the direction that the others went. They rushed through the forest until he could see Riley, August, and Yusuke up ahead, waving them forward. When they reached the team, Purdue made sure to take a quick moment to speak with August. Even with potential death flying over their heads, it was important to repair some of the damage his paranoia had caused. And he didn't want August to become another Galen, bitter and angry with him over differences.

While the others got ready to keep moving, Purdue led the giant man aside to have a private conversation. August looked at him with a mixture of worry, confusion, and with a bit of an 'I told you so' kind of face. And it was true, he had indeed told Purdue so.

"August...I was wrong for all of the utter shit I threw at you. Nonsense accusations...and all I did was make myself look like an ass."

"You've always been an ass," Nina cut in. Obviously, their conversation wasn't quite as private as Purdue hoped it was.

"That may be so," Purdue said over to her before lowering his volume and speaking directly to August again. "But I shouldn't have jumped to conclusions without more evidence to go off of. It was just...it's just been hard figuring out what's what since taking over the Black Sun."

"No worries," August said with a shrug of his broad shoulders. "It was just what those people up there in that chopper wanted. They wanted to see how we would all react."

"Aye," Purdue said, glancing up through the trees. "All of those bastards flying around must have had a real good laugh watching me. I'm sure I put on quite the show for them."

"I'm just glad I'm not prime suspect number one anymore."

"Case closed," Purdue said with some embarrassment. "I won't doubt you again."

"Good," August said, offering his hand. When Purdue took it, he squeezed Purdue's hand hard and continued. "If the day comes that I do betray you, I'll do it in a much more awesome way than any of that. Believe me, I wouldn't be slitting open old men in their sleep."

Purdue winced at the strong handshake before pulling away. "Comforting, thanks."

They returned back to the group who were all looking around nervously. They really should have been moving but Purdue was glad that he got to tidy things up with August. Now, though, it really was time to figure out an escape plan.

"So what do we do exactly?" Riley asked, never drawing her gaze away from the sky above. "We can't hide from them forever. Not when they're swooping around like a dragon."

"You're right," Purdue said. He tried to think of their best option but none of the options seemed like good choices.

"The only way we can really get away is by bringing that thing down."

His team looked understandably bewildered. They all knew that it was no easy task to bring down a helicopter, especially without any kinds of weapons but he did have one plan in mind. It seemed likely to fail but it might just be crazy enough to work. One thing Purdue had learned from traveling to the most dangerous places in the world for years was that there was always a way out, no matter how bleak or impossible the situation was. This wasn't any different...except that it could get very, very messy...

"You have a plan then? Right?" Yusuke asked, looking eager to get some vengeance for Shin Wo.

"Aye," Purdue smiled at them all but found very few smiles in return. "But you're all not going to like it...at all." He turned to August and tapped the big man's shoulder. "How is your throwing arm?"

17

HELICOPTER BLADES

Purdue walked out of the forest's tree line by himself, his arms raised high. He still held the bag of Genghis Khan's ones in one hand. The helicopter hovered in front of him and he could see that blond man in the trench coat sitting on the side of it. He put the megaphone to his mouth and spoke again.

"Am I going crazy or is that you, David Purdue? Finally coming around and seeing some sense? It's about damn time. Where are you friends?"

Purdue looked up at that man, and despite the distance, knew that they were locking eyes.

"Well come on over then!"

Purdue could have surrendered right then and there. He could have given himself over without any sort of fight. Maybe he would spare them all if Purdue cooperated, but there was just

228

as much of a chance that he would slaughter them all the second he got the bones, if not before.

"Bring me the bones, Purdue. Now."

Purdue had his own plans, and for those plans to work, he couldn't do that. He broke into a sprint to his left, racing away from the helicopter. He ran as fast as he could, making sure he didn't drop Genghis Khan's remains. He could hear the helicopter veer out of its idle hovering and then heard the voice yell out over the speakers again.

"What the hell do you think you're doing, Purdue?'

Purdue didn't look back. He just kept running, staring straight ahead. He could hear the helicopter blades spinning behind him, coming closer. He wouldn't be able to outrun it long but that wasn't the point now. He just needed that helicopter in just the right position. He ran past a hill, and waved his arm, giving the signal to spring his plan into action.

Purdue turned and faced the helicopter and the aircraft hovered over him.

"Really?" The man called over the megaphone. "What the hell even was that? Some piss poor escape attempt? Or just giving time for your friends to try to run? We'll catch them too. So what's the point of that?"

Purdue smiled. He had the helicopter exactly

where he wanted it to be. For the first time this entire expedition, he had the upper hand over these people that had manipulated all of their movements along the way. He was the one pulling the strings now, without them knowing it.

Now it was up to August—and he was right where he was supposed to be.

Purdue pointed past the helicopter and past the man inside with the megaphone. The man looked away from Purdue and turned to his right. The whole aircraft followed suit and tilted in the direction that Purdue was pointing so the pilots could get a better look.

August stood on the slope of a nearby hill, making him stand at a similar height to where the helicopter was hovering in the air. He held Galen's cane in his hand.

The thing about helicopters was that they were incredibly fragile vehicles. If one thing went even slightly wrong or one thing was knocked even a little off balance, the whole aircraft could be compromised.

August had spent this entire trip having his loyalty questioned and being looked at as a possible enemy, all because these men in the helicopter had manipulated the entire expedition. They were the ones that put him in such an uncomfortable situation and nearly destroyed his relationship with the other members of the Order of the Black Sun. August needed some redemption, and in this case, that also meant some retribution. He looked straight at the helicopter and saw that smug blond man sitting there, looking at him with confusion.

The megaphone clicked on and the man's voice called out, loud enough for everyone around them to hear. "And just what do you think you're...?"

August couldn't help but smile and he hoped that the man in the chopper saw it. He hoped that he saw just how happy he was to do this and would know that he was the wrong person to try to frame. August took Galen Fitzgerald's cane in his hand, gave it one last look, and then threw it at the helicopter with all of his strength. The walking stick shot through the air and smashed straight through the windshield of the helicopter. The pilot was knocked out on impact, leaning forward on the control panel.

The helicopter buckled off to one side unsteadily and the leader sitting there in the doorway of the transport looked shocked. He grabbed hold of a rigging inside the chopper to steady himself and his mouth fell open before the helicopter careened downward toward the ground below. They never saw it coming, and even if they did, they probably wouldn't have thought it would matter—but it did. August watched the helicopter spin out of control. The blades on top of it rattled against the rocks and snapped and the vehicle smashed down onto its side as smoke and fire rose up from it. Moments before, it was in the sky, in complete control of the situation, now its wings were clipped and the people inside had completely lost their advantage.

Purdue waved up to August and had never felt so grateful to have that behemoth on their side. He had wasted so much time questioning him, interrogating him, and accusing him of being nothing more than a traitor. Hopefully August could forgive him. He shouldn't have just jumped to conclusions but at that time, it had seemed so clear. It was a bad way to start a relationship between a boss and their worker, but Purdue was going to fix it. He was going to make sure that any bad blood they had between them was cleared up because it certainly was now from Purdue's end.

That was one hell of a shot that he made. No one else could have thrown that cane that hard or that accurately but those big arms August had sure came in handy. He may have come into this expedition as nothing more than muscle to have in case of an emergency, but that was exactly what they needed in the end.

Purdue walked toward the site of the helicopter crash. Hopefully, it was a hard enough hit to knock these bastards out of commission. Otherwise, they might not be completely in the clear yet. Pieces of the helicopter's blades were scattered about the area and the vehicle itself was all smashed in from its fall. Purdue peaked through the shattered cockpit window and it looked like both people in the front were dead as could be. He moved around the vehicle and that was when he saw him—that man that had shown up demanding Genghis Khan's bones.

That man was pinned inside of the crashed copter, the upper half of his body practically hanging out of it. He was bloody from the crash but he was blinking, still alive—good. Purdue wanted him alive. If he had died when the helicopter went down, that would have been fine since it meant Purdue and his team would live. Getting rid of him would have been a victory, but by him still being alive, there was a chance to learn just who he even was.

Purdue stepped in front of the wounded man, wanting to just tear him apart for this whole ambush of his, but refraining so he could go after him with his head instead of with his fists. Purdue took a step closer to the copter and glared down at him. The man looked up at Purdue but didn't look afraid. He actually kind of looked happy to see him. Still, this was the best time to get answers and that was what Purdue knew he had to do.

"Who do you work for? Galen?"

He had to ask, but he already knew the answer. There was no chance that Purdue's earlier theory was correct but he wanted it confirmed for good.

"That Irish guy? Didn't you see me shoot

him? Are you really that paranoid to think that that was some kind of act? How is he, by the way? I'm an excellent shot." The man stared laughing, even as he coughed up blood. His injuries from the crash couldn't dampen how funny that prospect was to him. "Does anyone actually work for him? No. Especially now that he's dead, dead, dead."

Purdue was surprised by how angry the taunts about Galen were making him, but it was infuriating to hear a murderer mock their victim. They had already done them the biggest insult by taking their life. There was no need to keep going after them after you had already killed them and ripped any chance away for them to defend themselves.

"Then who?"

"Wouldn't you like to know..." Purdue pressed down on the open gash in the man's shoulder and the laughing was replaced by pained grunts and growls. He bit back the pain and kept talking. "Careful, Purdue. We're already disappointed. Start torturing people and you'll look more and more like Julian Corvus. We would hate to see that the Order of the Black Sun hasn't really changed after all. We all hoped for more--"

"Who is we!?"

The man's gazed drifted to the fire on the ground. His expression sunk and he suddenly seemed very distant, lost in his own thoughts. His eyes were wide with dread. He didn't seem to care much about the wounds he had suffered anymore. He was far more concerned with whatever outcome he was playing out in his head.

"She is not going to be happy with me. That old crone is going to be furious. Furious..."

"Who!?" Purdue shouted.

There was a cracking sound behind the man's bloody lips and white foam oozed out of his mouth. His eyes rolled up and he started choking on the liquid that now flooded his maw.

A cyanide capsule.

Purdue grabbed at the man's jaw, in some futile attempt to save him from the poison but it was too late. The man collapsed back into the wreckage as the cyanide ate away at the last little bits of life he had left.

All of the answers and information he had were washed away by the cyanide, and died with him.

Purdue stood over the stranger, staring down at the fresh corpse. Who was this man? He couldn't have been part of the Order of the Black Sun...and apparently hadn't been working for Galen either. And all of those things had been saying his last moments.

We are disappointed.

She is not going to be happy.

Who was he talking about? Purdue thought that his days of facing mysterious groups of enemies would be over once he had the Black

Sun under his control. Evidently, he was mistaken. There was another player out there, and he had no idea what game they were even playing.

But there was someone who might.

18

THE DEMON IN THE BOX

The flight back to the Order of the Black Sun headquarters was long and quiet. They were all exhausted from the search. Everyone passed out from fatigue at least once on the flight. Purdue woke up from one of those periods of sleep to see everyone else with their eyes closed, breathing slowly. He was so proud of all of them for not only making it through such a surprisingly difficult expedition, but also proving just how beneficial they were to have on board his new vision for the Black Sun.

The bag of Genghis Khan's bones were in Purdue's lap. He usually would have felt awkward having a dead guy's remains in his arms while he slept but he didn't feel that at all. He just wanted to be sure that those bones were safe and he wasn't going to give them up until he was face to face with Elijah and ready to hand them over to be stored in the Black Sun's deep vaults. Those remains had been lost since their burial, since Genghis Khan's body had been carted away in the dead of night and buried after the slaughter of the slaves who prepared his resting place. Now they were found, they were out in the world.

Still, it was a bit gross to think he'd been holding someone's bones for so long.

Yusuke's eyes drifted open and he smirked at Purdue. He let out a yawn and then slowly walked over, taking the seat beside him. He looked like he was barely awake, but was self-aware enough to give Purdue a pat on the shoulder.

"You got him Purdue," Yusuke said with a quiet snicker. "You got the Great Khan. After eight hundred years, you were the one to get him."

"Stop flattering me," Purdue said. "We all found them. I'm just the one who pulled them out of the dirt."

"And put together the whole search," Yusuke said.

"Technically, that dead bastard with the helicopter put together search. I was just the ass that followed all the clues he laid out for me. The fish that took the bait and let himself get reeled in...but also the fish that then came up with the plan to kill that fishermen..." He wasn't sure his musings were making much sense with how tired he was, but he hoped Yusuke got the point. "This was a joint effort. Whether we were manipulated or not, we found Genghis Khan's tomb. We all did. Whoever that man worked for might have found them first, but as far as I'm concerned, they forfeited their bragging rights the second they put those bones back to trick us."

"Who do you think they were?" Yusuke asked.

"No one good, and I may have a way to find out."

Purdue continued to think about their attackers for the rest of the flight. Someone out there was powerful, and had enough resources to completely take control of Purdue's expedition for the tomb. Once he got back to the compound, he would try to learn more, but for now, all he could do was sit there in his seat, trying to figure out who this new enemy was.

PURDUE WAS glad to see Sam as he entered the compound. As much as he enjoyed the team he worked with and as much as he had grown to trust them through all of the trials and tribulations, he was so happy to see such a familiar face. He had felt a little guilty about leaving Sam behind. They had been on all kinds of adventures together and they had been side by side while trying to gain their lives back from Julian Corvus. They butted heads sometimes but usually made it through to the end together and on good terms. It must have been alarming to

Sam to be excluded from the search, but Purdue couldn't rely too much on his old friends. Having Nina there was one thing, but Sam being there too would only have been a crutch and he probably wouldn't have bonded with Riley, Yusuke, and August as well as he did. This was about new connections, not leaning on old ones, and it had proven successful at the end of the journey.

Sam approached, putting on a fake pout before breaking into a smile and holding out his hand, which Purdue happily took. Sam glanced down at the burlap sack in Purdue's grip. He pushed it partially open and looked down inside of it.

"Is that really him? Genghis Khan? He's shorter than I expected. Thinner too. And older. He looked so much younger in all of those paintings." As usual, Sam's delivery of humor was dry and he barely looked like he was even trying to kid around. Purdue was surprised how much he actually missed that type of talk while on this quest. "Really, are you sure you found the right guy?"

"Hilarious," Purdue said and pulled the bones away from Sam. He started walking toward the deep vault doors and Sam followed right on his heel. "Believe it or not, Sam, we really could have used you out there in retrospect."

"Really?" Sam looked unconvinced and was

still pretending to pout. "You guys found the tomb well enough."

That was true. It had been a success, but they could have used another semi-capable fighter to have tag along. August was strong and had more than proven that he could help protect the team and Purdue could hold his own in a fight. Even Nina had shown that she was capable in a pinch but Sam had been in more scraps than Purdue probably, so would have been helpful in that sense.

"We did, aye," Purdue said. "But not without incident and kicking over what might be a very big nest of bees. We'll see..."

"What do you mean?" Sam perked up with some worry. "How big of a nest? Bigger than us? Bigger than the Black Sun?"

"Maybe," Purdue said. "I'm actually hoping to find out now."

Sam glanced from Purdue to the giant deep vault doors ahead and the cogs in his head were very clearly turning. His face contorted into a mix of confusion and anger. "Please tell me you're going to be going through the files to find out...and not..."

"The latter one," Purdue said without even letting Sam finish. "And before you bite my head off...it's the best idea we have. The only one who might actually know what we're dealing with."

"But you can't trust him--"

"You don't think I know that?" Purdue

couldn't help but laugh. "I know exactly who I'm going to be talking with. That bastard ruined my life, remember? No one is going to be more careful talking to him than I am."

"Well then I'm talking to him with you."

"No," Purdue said firmly. He didn't putting himself at risk even talking to Julian again. He didn't want to put anyone else in that situation. "You're going to stay out here. It's going to be a private conversation between us."

"And is that an order, great leader?" Sam asked, folding his arms.

"It is," Purdue said entirely seriously. "Elijah will be out here in a minute or two too. You can be pissed off with him if you like, but I'm talking to Julian. Just me."

Purdue put his hand on the scanner and the thick doors of the deep vaults pulled themselves open. He glanced at Sam as he entered and could see the frustration on his friend's face. He was just leaving him behind again, but it was for his own good. There was no need to endanger anyone but himself. The doors shut behind him and he could still practically feel Sam's frustration seeping through them. Sam was going to be pissed off for a while about this, but he would get over it. He could deal with Sam being upset instead of dead. It was a good enough trade.

Elijah approached to greet him but Purdue knew he could save the small talk for later. He handed the curator the bag of Genghis Khan's bones and asked for him to go outside until he came out. Elijah took the bones but looked just as confused as Sam. He pushed his glasses up his nose and looked in the direction that Purdue was going to be heading, knowing exactly what he was thinking.

"I don't think you want to do this..." Elijah said uneasily. "I haven't even gone off there...and I spend all day, every day in this place."

"Aye, you're right."

Elijah was right. Purdue didn't want to do this. He never wanted to have to be in this position, certainly not so soon. It was something he had promised himself he wouldn't do but they were out of options. This was the best way for him to get some sort of answers.

Once Elijah was gone, Purdue walked through the deep vault room, glancing at all of the relics he had collected, sitting in their glass containers. There were so many memories kept in those display cases, locked safely away in this high tech vault that the Black Sun had. They were far safer than they had been when they were stolen from him, hopefully safe enough to never be taken again.

Those weren't the displays he was there for, though. He was looking for a much larger display case than any of those, one that had much more different contents than the rest of them. He walked straight up to the tall box shape in the corner of the room, the shape that was shrouded by curtains running down its length, hiding what was inside.

He really, really didn't want to do this. He would have preferred to be anywhere else in that moment. There were just too many unanswered questions, things that he wanted to know but didn't even have the slightest idea of where to start looking for them. He needed a second opinion, a second pair of eyes that was more knowledgeable on what he was looking for.

This was the only way.

The curtains draped over the sheets of reinforced glass fell away and Purdue saw his greatest enemy for the first time in a while.

Julian Corvus sat in the display case that was serving as his holding cell. Purdue thought it was the right place to put an immortal man like him, among all of the rest of the world's oddities. The impenetrable vault that protected the other artifacts served just as well as a prison that would be impossible for Julian to break free from. He would last forever in that glass box, never starve or dehydrate or even fall prey to disease. Thanks to his immortality, it would be everlasting imprisonment. It was what that bastard deserved for nearly destroying Purdue's life beyond repair.

His icy gray eyes looked up from where he sat.

"Mr. Purdue...and what brings the wise and powerful leader of the Order of the Black Sun to my humble abode? I don't believe I am worthy of such a prestigious honor." Julian managed a thin little smile, but there was no joy forming it. There was nothing but malice. "What's the old saying...heavy is the head that wears the crown. So tell me, Mr. Purdue, how much does your neck hurt?"

"Much less now that I kicked out everyone in the order that would have wanted to strangle me. It's been a much more pleasant place now that you're not controlling everything and everyone. The Order of the Black Sun was always bad. You just made it so much worse somehow. But now it can actually be a group dedicated to doing good for the world."

"I would have done plenty of good for the world but you just had to keep ruining everything..."

"You tried to become a god. I highly doubt that would have been good. A psychopath shouldn't be the leader of anything. Not the Order of the Black Sun, and definitely not the leader of everyone else on this rock, aye?"

The little smile that was on Julian's face went away. He wasn't even going to pretend to be cordial now.

"Why even come here?" Julian hissed bitterly. "Have you just come to gloat? Is that it? Come to admire your greatest trophy?"

"No," Purdue said bluntly. "And you are far from the best trophy I have." He glanced around at the other artifacts on display. "You didn't even make the top fifty."

"Then why?"

"I just have a few questions to ask you, Julian. That's all."

"And you expect me to answer them? Why should I?"

"Because you have nothing better to do."

Julian didn't look like he could argue with that point. "I suppose that is true. Go on then."

Purdue started recounting what happened with their mysterious assailant. He left out details about the actual expedition that they were on, though. There was no need to tell Julian that much. He just needed to tell him enough to hopefully get some answers.

"He seemed to know a lot about the order. He kept using the word 'we' and he mentioned some old crone, that's how he put it. He said she wasn't going to be happy with him before he bit down on cyanide and that was the end of our conversation."

Julian's icy gray eyes seemed to shine a little brighter now. His lips curled into another small knowing smirk. Julian slowly rose to his feet, running the tips of his fingers against the glass membrane between them as he stood up. He clearly knew something, just like Purdue thought. Now it was just a matter of getting him to share what he knew.

"Fascinating. I should have expected as

much." Julian showed that demented grin that sometimes pulled apart his face. "Didn't I warn you?"

Purdue didn't appreciate being teased. Julian knew damn well that he hadn't said anything about anyone else in the game.

"You didn't warn me about shit."

Julian ran his finger in a circular motion along his glass confinements.

"Oh, I suppose I didn't..." Julian's sick grin never left his face now. He was back where he liked to be in—in control of the situation. He pressed his palm against the glass and leaned forward as much as he could inside of there. That chilling gaze of his fixed on Purdue, bearing into him. "Look at you. You're so proud of being an expert on history...but you know so little about the history of this order. Next to nothing. You probably should have done some research before so callously taking my job."

Purdue hated letting Julian have even an iota of power over him, but he didn't have a choice right now. Julian very clearly had the information that he wanted but information was a powerful tool, and it gave Julian an undeniable edge over him at the moment. Purdue didn't care about this tug of war for power. He just wanted answers.

"Who are they?"

Julian relished every second of this and he didn't rush to give any answers. He was savoring the moment, looking at Purdue with pity like he was a child who didn't know anything. That was how Purdue felt, even. He felt stupid for not having made sure that he wasn't missing anything important when he became leader of the order. Even Julian, who had butchered his way into command had known about whatever threat this was.

"Let me out of this cage and I will gladly tell you all about the old lady."

That was it—Julian's power play. This was the moment he had probably been waiting for his entire time inside of that display case. He wanted Purdue to show a brief moment of weakness that he could exploit, and here it was. He might have even known that this strange group would come, and was just waiting for it to happen before trying to make a move, withholding sharing any information until the time was right. And now, he had leverage and he was making use of it.

"That's not going to happen," Purdue said firmly.

"How sadistic of you, Mr. Purdue. Robbing me of basic human rights. No food. No water. I can't exactly stretch my legs inside of this box...throw me in a cell, at least. Some place where I could take a few steps. Lay on a bed. Anything."

"No." He wouldn't let Julian win, not after it took all of that time and effort to finally beat him. He finally had him contained and kept away from hurting anyone else. He wouldn't release him for anything. He couldn't. "No, you're going to stay right where you are. I'd love to know what you know...but if you don't feel like sharing...then you don't have to. I'll find out from someone else, or just wait for this crone and whoever else wants to take a shot to show up."

Julian suddenly smacked his hand against the glass, showing a quick flash of anger. That was his way. He was good at keeping up a calm, controlled demeanor until things started not going the way he wanted them to. Then the vicious demon beneath would come out.

"You need me! You need what I know!"

"Then spit it out, you bastard!" Purdue shouted back. He was sick of Julian's games and he was sick of having to even speak to him. This was already more conversation than he ever wanted to have with him. "Spit it out and maybe I'll consider letting you stretch your legs at some point."

Purdue turned away and moved for the rope to pull the curtains back up over the glass cage. He would love to know whatever Julian was hiding but he had no qualms with just putting Julian away forever and ending this.

Julian's desperation showed all over his face, and his hand squeaked against the glass as he slid it down his cage. He tapped his brow against the glass wall between them and ground his teeth in frustration.

"The old lady is not someone you want to meet."

Purdue was surprised that Julian even said anything at all.

"You may have prided yourself as the Order of the Black Sun's greatest enemy, Purdue...but that wasn't entirely true. You were just the one that we knew it was at least possible to defeat."

"And you couldn't even do that," Purdue chimed in. "So this old lady is an enemy of the order. What's her name?"

"I don't know," Julian said. "I've never known. No one does. But I do know this...if you have upset her, then she will come. And when she does, you don't stand a chance. None of you do."

"Very cryptic...I need specifics."

Julian sat back down in his glass box.

"I've told you what you need to know, and considering this is your fault, be thankful I even told you that much."

"My fault?"

"I had plans in place when I was leader...plans that would have continued to protect us from the old lady's wrath. Those plans were squashed the moment you took the Black Sun from me."

"You mean the moment I kicked your ass, aye."

Julian ignored him.

"Thanks to you, the Order of the Black Sun will be finished soon enough. It was bad enough with you in charge but now...there will be nothing left at all. You want more information than that? Then you better release me."

Purdue started pulling the rope that heaved the curtains back over the glass cage. As the curtains started rising and blocking his view of Julian, he stopped.

"You're really not going to tell me more?"

"No," Julian hissed. "Not until I am out of this box...and by then, it may be too late. The old lady might have already destroyed everything. Good luck, Mr. Purdue. You were always ill fit to lead the order. I hope you can see that now. Do try to enjoy the last moments you have."

Purdue was sick of hearing Julian so he pulled the curtains completely up over the glass cage, draping it over and obscuring Julian from view.

This old lady sounded like some scary story, but Purdue wasn't afraid. He wasn't going to let some spooky tale get into his head. For all he knew, all of Julian's cryptic warnings were nothing more than fairy tales to give Purdue a reason to release him. Or maybe, it was all true. Either way, Purdue wasn't going to let himself get freaked out by it.

Whatever was coming, whoever this old lady was, and whatever her beef with the Black Sun was—Purdue would find a way to handle it, and he would do that without having to grovel to the man he hated most.

19

THE BLACK SUN'S NEW FLAMES

The team that had found Genghis Khan's tomb were all gathered around and Purdue was struggling to even figure out what to say to them. This was supposed to be something that wasn't too, too stressful. It was supposed to just be a standard mission that they could all tackle together, to build bonds, and get to know one another. It was meant to unite both the old and the new. It was meant to mend old wounds. It was meant to give them all a common goal to achieve together. They had done that—but it was far from an easy trip.

They all looked a bit shell shocked. Nina looked the most well put together, but she had been through worse than the rest of them before. She had gone through a lot of dangerous adventures with Purdue and recently had managed to survive a long imprisonment. If anything, she just looked let down that they had almost been killed again. She could probably have done with a much less eventful search.

Yusuke looked tired and stressed; none of his old expeditions probably went so poorly before and probably didn't involve so much violence and death. He might be regretting joining the Order of the Black Sun altogether. On his own, he had never been chased down by a helicopter that was trying to murder him. The Black Sun was supposed to make things easier for him, not harder. Hopefully, this wasn't enough to spook him, but Purdue wouldn't blame him if it was. If Yusuke wanted to leave the order now and go back to his successful solo career, Purdue would understand. There would be no bad blood over something like that. They were both professionals when it came to traveling the world in search of lost relics, but that didn't mean they were both meant for the way Purdue's expeditions turned out.

Riley was somehow still smiling, but that smile was much less bright than it had been at the start of all of this. The jokes and sarcastic remarks were still being thrown but they weren't quite as frequent as before. There was a lull between them sometimes and in those moments, he could see her bubbly personality start to crack. That bright light she gave off was dimmer but it was still enough to light up a room if need be. Purdue wondered if those visions of butchered slaves on top of that plateau were going to haunt her as badly as he knew they were going to stick with him. Sleep would be difficult for him for some time, and maybe it would be hard for her too. He hoped it wasn't too bad. She deserved some rest after this ordeal.

Then there was August. That mountain of a man wasn't the same suspicious brute that Purdue had seen him as when they first set out on this venture. He was battered, bruised, and bloodied from his fight with Oniel and from all of the action he had seen. He knew that August was looking for some excitement and maybe the chance to crack some skulls but this was probably more than he had ever expected or wanted. When he had been an enforcer for Julian Corvus, he must have been used to being in control and being the one dishing out the pain. This time, he spent a lot of that time on the run, under duress, or taking some hard hits himself. Still, throughout all of it, he had more than earned Purdue's trust. He wasn't just a blunt, muscular instrument and he certainly wasn't the conniving and calculating traitor that Purdue had accused him of being. He was a good man, loyal to a fault, who was willing to get his hands dirty if need be.

Purdue himself didn't feel the same as he had at the start of this, especially now knowing that there was another mysterious force out there trying to mess with his tenure as leader of the

Black Sun. All of this had been a strange experience full of growing pains as well as actual pains, but he had made it through. And despite how worn out his team looked, he was proud of all of them and elated that they had all made it through alive.

Now it was just a matter of what came next; that was still a discussion.

"So," Purdue broke the silence as they all sat around the table. "Was it everything you expected it to be?"

They all looked to one another awkwardly, like no one could decide who should even answer that question. Nina looked like she wanted to respond but would prefer that one of the newer members who had never been through this would voice their experience.

"Not exactly," Yusuke finally said. "I knew that your adventures were something to behold but this...I didn't realize how often you got yourself into situations where you were going to die...and somehow are still alive."

Purdue let out a little chuckle. "Escaping near-death has become something of a bad habit for me. One might even call it a skill, aye? This one wasn't the most dangerous trip I've been on, but it was up there at times. Especially since August was waiting to put a knife in my back the whole time." August shifted in his seat, frustrated, and opening his mouth to start defending himself but Purdue waved him down and smiled. "I'm only kidding, big man. I know, I know. You never would have used a knife."

August raised a brow but then the enormous man settled a little, nodding and even offering a smirk. He really was a teddy bear once you got to know him and got past the fact that he looked like some sort of human bulldozer ready to plow through everything and everyone.

"Well, I had fun," Riley said, throwing her hands up in a lazy shrug. "Most fun I've had in years. Maybe even ever."

There it was. He saw her expression falter just a little in between her jokes.

"I could have done without the crazy guy with the helicopter chasing us through the forest," Nina said. "Have we figured out who exactly that even was yet? That would make things a lot easier if we even knew anything at all."

"I spoke with Julian..."

Nina was immediately beside herself, her jaw practically on the floor. "Why would you do that?"

"Easy, love," Purdue said with some nervousness. He knew she wouldn't like that he had communicated with him, especially after everything he put her through. She would have preferred that he just stay in that box, with the curtain draped over it, and never had any interaction with the outside world ever again. She didn't want to risk anyone even talking to him. He understood her misgivings about it, but he hoped she would forgive him and understand why it had to be done. "The Order of the Black Sun has history with whoever our helicopter killer was and whoever he was working for. So I just had a few questions for my predecessor, that's all."

"You know you can't trust anything he says," Nina said frantically. "You can't."

"I don't," Purdue said firmly. "Believe me, but I still felt like I needed to hear what he had to say. Any information at all, even if I had to take it was a huge bloody grain of salt, was going to be worth it."

Nina scoffed and folded her arms, far more angry than she had ever been during the expedition for Genghis Khan's tomb; so much so, that the others looked shocked by seeing this side of her. Usually, she was so helpful, cooperative— maybe somewhat stubborn—but she didn't usually show so much raw anger. Purdue hoped that they shared his understanding of where this was coming from. Her anger was justified, but he needed her to see past it at the bigger picture.

She shook her head and then let out a long exhale in defeat. "And what did he say then?"

"Not much unfortunately," Purdue said. "Just some scary bedtime shit about an old lady that has some bad relationship with the order. Apparently, we should all be very afraid of her, but he didn't know anything else about her."

"Maybe we should be," Yusuke chimed in. "If

that man was just working for her, then she obviously has a long reach. It completely caught us off guard, didn't it? Even you, didn't it, Purdue?"

Purdue nodded and spoke honestly. "It did. Completely. I had no idea these people existed. I thought our troubles were done with Julian...or even just a few old grudges with people like Galen. Stragglers like some of the other people that quit when I took control of the order. Those were the only people I thought would be a little bit of a problem. But I had no idea that there was another big player out there...and I didn't even know we were playing any games with them."

Once again, the team looked uneasy. They were all staring into an enormous ocean, realizing that they weren't swimming alongside the biggest fish like they thought they were. There was something maybe even bigger out there, or at least something that posed an actual threat. The Order of the Black Sun might not be the most powerful organization dealing with ancient relics after all.

It had started Purdue even, learning that he had spent so long thinking that the Order of the Black Sun was the biggest enemy in his way. He thought beating them would be his greatest victory and doing so would bring about a much more peaceful world. Things were supposed to be better now, but instead, the Black Sun's fall and restructure had just exposed that there was something worse that was hiding in the background, waiting in the wings.

"So what do you think?" Purdue asked, addressing everyone as a collective. "You've done much more than dip your toes in to test the waters now. Without really planning to, you've all now taken the full plunge into this shit storm, aye? Now my question is...are you willing to stay afloat in this crap pile or would you prefer to step on out to find someplace cleaner?" They all looked at him with some confusion and he rolled his eyes. "What I am really trying to say is, did all of this scare you off or are you willing to continue? I can't promise that it's going to get better. If this fairy tale about this old lady is true, there's a chance this might actually get a lot worse. Are you ready for that?"

Nina—who had still looked like she wanted to rip Purdue's head off for talking to Julian—softened somewhat and even offered a small smile. Her choice was obvious enough. They'd been through too much together. If she was going to be scared off, it would have happened a long, long time ago.

Riley giggled to herself and then just clapped her hands together. "Hell yes. When's the next one?"

Yusuke seemed to think it over but slowly nodded. "I would like to continue, yes. We found Genghis Khan's remains. If we can do that...then I would love to be there to see what else the Order of the Black Sun is capable of."

Purdue felt a surge of relief come over him. They were two of his newest recruits and two of the ones that he liked the most. He wanted them to be part of this, and he wanted them to enjoy being a part of this, but it was hard to know if they actually would enjoy being members of the Black Sun. To hear that they were willing to keep going, even after some of the scares they had, made him so happy. He didn't want them to put themselves in danger again, no, but he did want to be working with people like them to change the world.

Lastly, August just put his elbows on the table, laced his big fingers together and leaned his bald head against his hands. He stared at the table for a minute before his gaze drifted back up to Purdue. He wasn't brand new to the order but he was new to this new version of it. He had it the worst of everyone on this expedition too, so it was impossible to know just where his head was at. Maybe he was still a bit pissed with Purdue or maybe he wasn't a big fan of the changes that had been made with Purdue as leader. It was a tense few seconds of silence before he spoke up.

"It really depends, man...do you trust me?"

Purdue didn't even have to think about it at this point. He was ashamed he had ever had to before. "I do. Completely."

"Good," August said and smiled. "Then I'm

in...as long as you're not accusing me of murder every time we go out looking for old shit."

"I'll refrain from pointing my fingers again."

August looked pleased with rubbing it in Purdue's face that he was never his enemy. He was going to make sure that Purdue didn't forget how wrong he was and he did it all with a very satisfied and shiny, white smile. "Yeah, no more pointing fingers...if you do, I'll make sure that I break them."

This was his team. He loved working with Nina and Sam. He would always work with them when it felt right or when he needed their expertise but one thing his new Order of the Black Sun needed was new blood and this squad that somehow survived such a messy quest were exactly like the kind of injection of life that was needed. They were the future, and they were going to help him protect history and protect the world from some of the worse secrets the past had to offer.

The Order of the Black Sun wasn't going anywhere—and they were going to be better than ever before.

———

ONCE EVERYONE HAD LEFT the room, Purdue found himself alone again. His heart was still full from the feeling that he had a core group that was going to help shepherd the future. He was happier than he had been in some time.

He had lost everything; his money, his relics, his friends, and his home. Now, he had all of those things back in one way or another and had taken measures to try and never let that happen again once he took the proverbial throne of the Black Sun. He had been in such a dark, hopeless place and never expected to be able to recover from. He had been begging on the streets, making deals with modern day pirates, and relying on nothing but an old witch book and his own intellect. Now, it all seemed so far behind him. It was another life, almost.

Some hadn't been able to move on from the past—Galen and Oniel had held onto those grudges until close to the very end. They had been stuck in the way things were, not willing to adapt, or change to things happening around them. They were hellbent on destroying Purdue for the slights that he had dealt them. The worst part was, he never felt like it was his fault for any of the things they hated him for. The two of them —Oniel especially—were dangerous individuals that were willing to resort to murder to get what they wanted. They hated him for not letting them get what they wanted, and Purdue didn't feel guilty about that. He enjoyed stopping psychopaths and megalomaniacs from achieving their dreams. Who cares if it made him a few enemies here and there?

Still, those last moments with Galen dying next to that tree had stuck with him. As much as he and the Irishman butted heads, it was unfortunate how it all turned out. If only they could have just had a civil discussion or debate instead of Galen trying so hard to humiliate him or murder him all the time. He was never his friend and Galen was never the nemesis that he seemed to think he was. In the end, Galen was just a man who had some insecurities and there was nothing Purdue could really do to help him.

Purdue pulled out a book that he had refused to read for years, Galen's self-indulgent autobiography, *Guns, Glaives, and Guinness: The Many Adventures of Galen Fitzgerald*. Purdue had never had any interest in reading it. It was sure to just be Galen stroking his own ego and telling very skewed versions of the truth. Galen was a rich but incompetent man when it came to his archaeological prowess. He failed far more than he succeeded but he doubted that the novel would agree with that statistic. Even so, it felt like the right thing to do to finally read it.

He opened up the book and within the first few lines closed it. It was more than enough for him. He had hoped to get further but there had only ever been so much Galen Fitzgerald that he could take. Galen wouldn't have cared if he actually read it, not really; he probably would have been pleased that Purdue even spent the money to buy it.

The one lingering itch that Purdue had about Galen was the Spear of Destiny. It was the artifact that had made their cross for the most significant time, the search that led to the complete schism between them and that had made Galen's jealousy and animosity toward Purdue boil to the surface. It was an important relic to history but also an important part of Purdue's recent history. It was what had revived Julian Corvus, earned him his place as tyrannical leader of the Black Sun, and been part of what killed Charles.

The Spear of Destiny was too important to both the world and to Purdue's own life to just leave around without an owner now. It was also too dangerous to let fall into the wrong hands again. So, on a rainy day, Purdue would find out where Galen put it and he'd reclaim that spear. Maybe he would exchange it for the god awful autobiography he had just tried and failed to read.

Julian was defeated and now Galen was dead. A new team of young blood had succeeded.

The past was the past. Purdue was glad to be settling old scores, putting old grudges to rest, and finding better ways forward.

Then there was the matter of that mysterious shadow organization stalking them...he would have to worry about that another day, once they could learn more about them. Until then, he would just keep trying to make the Order of the Black Sun even better, for as long as he could.

EPILOGUE

THE WISDOM OF THE ELDERLY

The old lady's chair creaked and its swaying halted immediately. Once again, she found herself surprised. It used to be such a rare thing but the recent events kept catching her off guard and all of those surprises came from an even more surprising source—that spoiled Scotsman, David Purdue. He just kept doing things that she never would expect someone like him to do. The way he dealt with Julian Corvus and the Order of the Black Sun was surprisingly effective and his transition into the order's leader was just as successful somehow. She thought that some of the older members would have enacted a mutiny by now but somehow, he remained. That was a problem.

The Order of the Black Sun had been through a number of leaders but she preferred when it was the old men sitting around their wooden table. They were easy to manipulate, wrapped around her finger. Then the upstart Julian Corvus had taken over, a legitimate madman who wouldn't be controlled but also knew better than to try and go against her and her own plans. David Purdue hadn't even known about her, so she needed to make sure he was aware of the kind of power they wielded. She had expected to help him find his treasure, show him that they had allowed it to happen, and then he would submit. Instead, he had killed one of her favorite helpers.

Maddox was an effective tool but he did sometimes go overboard. He probably got himself into the mess he ended up in, but she wouldn't allow his death to go unanswered. David Purdue and his new Order of the Black Sun were responsible, whether they wanted to be or not. She would make sure that they would pay for the blow they had dealt her.

She had files brought to her, so many files, on everything that the world knew about David Purdue. It was important to know everything about a new player on the board. He had been an enemy of the Black Sun for so long, but never a threat to her, never even aware of her. Now, in his new role as the Black Sun's leader, he was actually worth noticing—and he was already aggravating. She could see why he had been such a thorn in the previous iteration of the Black Sun's side. She could also see why he had somehow flipped the tables and was now running the organization that had spent so long trying to get rid of him.

David Purdue was already an annoyance—and he was very quickly becoming a problem.

The most important thing that the old lady had learned in her nine decades on the planet was that if there was a problem in your way, it was best to get rid of it as soon as possible. With that mindset, she had spent all of those many, many years with very few problems, at least not many that remained problems for long. She had a nice, easy life without much stress at all, because anything that might stress was immediately removed.

David Purdue would be removed, and the Order of the Black Sun would either fall back in line or would be decimated.

Her chair rocked back and forth at a quicker pace than it had in days.

She smiled.

This was going to be more fun than she had in decades—at least for her.

The Order of the Black Sun would not be enjoying themselves.

Made in the USA
San Bernardino, CA
04 April 2020